VOICE
IN
THE
NIGHT

Also by Velda Johnston

VOICE IN THE NIGHT

Velda Johnston

DODD, MEAD & COMPANY, New York

Published by Dodd, Mead & Company, Inc.
79 Madison Avenue, New York, N.Y. 10016
Distributed in Canada by
McClelland and Stewart Limited, Toronto
Manufactured in the United States of America
First Edition

Library of Congress Cataloging in Publication Data

Johnston, Velda.
    Voice in the night.

    I. Title.
PS3560.0394V6   1984   813'.54   84-1597
ISBN 0-396-08379-X

For MILDRED BROWN,
and also for EUGENIA HUMPHRIES

VOICE
IN
THE
NIGHT

1

WHEN I first fled my hometown with my small daughter, I put at least some trust in the folk wisdom that says that the memory of an event, however horrifying, will in time lose its power to overwhelm. But in my case that had not proved to be true. Even after I'd spent four years in Manhattan, a sudden guilty memory of my husband's death still could shatter me.

And it was not just in my darkened bedroom that I would be assailed by a vision of Neil in his last moments of life, face turning toward me with an expression of blended hatred and pleading. It also could happen to me in a place as noisy and brightly lighted as my neighborhood supermarket.

On that particular late afternoon in February, the A & P a block from my Upper East Side apartment was thronged with its usual after-five customers. These were not the sort of shoppers I had encountered three years earlier when, too short of money

1

to leave town for my vacation, I had done my grocery buying in the morning hours. Those shoppers had been housewives, some with curlers lumpy beneath their head scarves as they made their leisurely choices of roasting chickens or legs of lamb or stewing beef. But early evening brought a change of tempo here, as it does everywhere in New York. Now the broad aisles were crowded with the single, the smartly dressed, the upwardly striving, just released from their desks in Wall Street brokerage firms, Madison Avenue advertising agencies, and the executive suites of Fifth Avenue department stores. As they made their swift selections of lamb chops and yoghurt and romaine lettuce, their faces under the bleak fluorescent lights still bore signs of the intense daily struggle that enabled them to live in this expensive neighborhood. About a third of them were men. And several of the women, including me, obviously were single mothers, accompanied by offspring picked up from schools and day care centers.

At the fruit and vegetable counter my six-year-old Melissa asked, "Can we buy some grapes? Can we, Mama?"

I looked at the posted price and shuddered. "Not unless I win a lottery. Besides, we have applesauce in the freezer."

"I hate applesauce!"

My daughter, it goes without saying, is my heart's darling. She also can be on occasion a pain in the neck, especially if my neck already aches from a day spent bending over manuscripts.

2

"We used to buy grapes," Melissa argued. "Why can't we—"

"That was last summer. Grapes were cheaper then. Now they come from faraway places, and so they cost a lot."

"What faraway places?"

"Oh, I don't know! Somewhere around the Mediterranean Sea, perhaps."

"What's the Metter—Metter—"

"Oh, Melissa! Don't ask me such questions now. I'll show you on the map when we get home."

I became aware that a blond young woman stood a few feet away from me at the counter, flat tan briefcase tucked under one arm, her hand clasping that of a boy a year or so younger than Melissa. She smiled at me. It was a sisterly smile, both ruefully amused and proud. It seemed to say, "It's hell sometimes, but we do manage, don't we?"

I smiled back at her, warmed by the thought that we were legion, we young women hoisting ourselves up the career ladder with one hand while cradling a child in the other arm.

But just then a green-smocked youth, watering can in hand, appeared at the counter and bathed those mounds of jewellike—and almost jewel-priced—purple grapes in a fine mist. A few drops of the spray reached my face.

Instantly I was back there on that riverbank in Arizona, with a wind blowing moisture toward me off the foaming rapids. I saw Neil's face turning toward me as the water swept him downstream, a white face in which terror blended with fury.

The sense of sisterhood the young woman's smile had bestowed upon me vanished. The things I had in common with her and the other young mothers around me were as nothing compared to the terrible event which set me apart. Oh, nearly all of them, especially the divorced ones, must have a few painful memories of the men to whom they had once been married. But not one of them, I was sure, had to live with the thought that she perhaps was responsible for the death of her child's father.

Almost blindly I reached out, grasped a lemon, and placed it in the wheeled basket which already held my bulging briefcase, a bunch of spinach, and a plastic-wrapped package of chicken thighs. With my daughter trailing me, I wheeled the basket to the checkout counter. By the time I reached the woman cashier it was completely dark outside, making the plate-glass windows huge mirrors for the patient lines of customers and the food-laden stacks behind them.

Handing me my change, the cashier said idiotically, "Have a nice day," and I replied, with equal idiocy, "Thank you. You too."

Melissa and I emerged onto Lexington Avenue. Its broad sidewalk was piled high with supermarket delivery crates, and the street beyond was clogged with rush-hour traffic. The air felt raw, but to my relief there was no sign of the snow the Weather Bureau had predicted. When we reached our apartment house, I was relieved also to see that only one person, an elderly woman who lived on the second floor, was waiting for the elevator.

Although our fifty-year-old building was well constructed, its elevator was underpowered. If too many people crowded into it, its upward progress slowed to an almost imperceptible crawl. Terrified that it might stop between floors, I would go into the sort of claustrophobic panic that has afflicted me ever since, at the age of five, I was locked in a clothes closet by my ten-year-old cousin Mahlon. But however crowded, the elevator never had stopped entirely, not when I was in it, and I think I had always managed to hide my anxiety from my fellow passengers. Tonight, though, especially after that traumatic memory which had assailed me in the A & P, I was glad that the elevator would carry only the three of us. The woman got off at the second floor, and Melissa and I rode up to the eighth.

As often happened when I unlocked my front door, I reflected how lucky we were to have this place. Less than a month after Melissa and I had arrived in New York, I had sublet the apartment, furnished, from a Mr. and Mrs. Witterall, a retired couple who planned to spend the summer with relations in England. Perhaps they figured that a two-year-old would be less destructive of their unimaginative but fairly expensive furniture than some party-giving single or young couple. Anyway, they let me have the place. Thanks to the fact that the Witteralls had lived there for thirty years, the rent was reasonable indeed by Manhattan standards, less

5

than half of the thirty-five dollars a day I had been paying for a somewhat frowzy hotel room in Midtown.

Near the end of that summer the Witteralls wrote that they had decided to stay in England permanently. If I wanted to buy their furniture and take over the lease, their New York lawyer would arrange the transaction. Of course I jumped at the offer, even though buying the furniture would take nearly every cent I had in the bank.

Since then I had signed two new leases, each at an increase in rent. Nevertheless, I still had a remarkable bargain—an Upper East Side, two-bedroom apartment, only a block and a half from Melissa's school.

I changed to jeans and an old sweater and cooked our dinner of broiled chicken, herbed potatoes, and spinach.

As we sat in the dining nook Melissa asked, "Mama, what's a holy terror?"

I looked at my daughter. Like me, she has sherry-colored eyes and hair of almost the same red-brown shade. Thank God, there is nothing in her appearance to remind me of her father. Her behavior sometimes reminds me of Neil's, but that is only because she is a child, something that Neil continued to be even at the age of twenty-eight.

"That depends," I said. "Why do you ask?"

"Sister Mary Joseph called a girl a holy terror."

Sister Mary Joseph was the first-grade teacher at the school which had accepted my daughter, even though we are not Catholic. "Why did Sister Mary

Joseph call this girl a holy terror?"

"Because she was running and yelling in the play street."

I knew what she meant. During certain hours of the day the street where Melissa's school stands is barred, between Park and Madison Avenues, to all motor traffic, so that the children will have a safe place to play at noon and during recess. Usually the racket can be heard for a quarter of a mile in any direction. But on days when the Weather Bureau classifies the city's air as unhealthful, the nuns forbid their charges to scream or run, lest they take additional pollution into their small lungs.

That rule, like all the school's rules, is strictly enforced. In fact, the institution's reputation for firm discipline was one of the reasons I had been so happy to enroll my enchanting but strong-willed child in it. The other reasons were its nearness to our apartment, and the fact that the children of working mothers could remain on the premises until five-thirty.

"Which girl did she say was a holy terror?"

"Just a girl in my class."

"It was you, wasn't it?"

After a moment the red-brown head nodded.

"Melissa, you mustn't try to fib."

"I didn't fib," my small Jesuitical reasoner answered. "I said it was a girl in my class. I'm a girl in my class."

"Eat your chicken."

Moments later the phone rang. Mike, I thought, my pulse quickening with mingled hope and apprehension. I went into my bedroom to answer it.

Mike said, "How are you, Carla?"

"Fine. Just fine."

He was silent for a moment. I could picture him in his apartment across town, long body stretched out on his bed, phone to his ear, rough dark brown hair shining in the lamplight. Wonderful, thoroughly grown-up Mike, whom I'd been in love with almost ever since we'd met eight months earlier.

"I'm going up to Vermont next weekend. Will you come with me?"

It was the question I had both feared and longed to hear.

"Mike, after last time—"

"Except for that one episode, the last time was wonderful. You know that as well as I do."

Yes, I knew it. I had left Melissa with Dodie Sims, an artist friend whose two Siamese cats and large fund of riddles were an endless source of delight to my daughter. On snowbanked roads Mike and I had driven north through Connecticut and Massachusetts to the gleaming white mountains and pine-fragrant air and church-steepled villages of Vermont. As Mike had said, it had all been wonderful. The cold air rushing past on the slopes. The crackling fire in the dining room of the inn where we stayed. The slanted-ceilinged bedroom where, for the first time in my life, I learned how glorious lovemaking could be, not just for the body but for something else—heart, or spirit, or whatever you want to call it.

But on our second night at the inn, I dreamed

8

of Neil's death. As in all dreams, many circumstances were altered. Instead of afternoon sunlight, the landscape was bathed in darkness, although that did not keep my dreaming self from seeing everything that happened. And in the dream Neil wore, not a checked sport shirt and chinos and paratrooper-style boots, but the dinner jacket in which he had appeared so dazzling to my nineteen-year-old gaze the first time he had taken any notice of me. What was more, the stream into which he toppled drunkenly from a boulder was not blue and foam flecked, but black and shiny, like some gigantic serpent. But the face he turned toward me was filled, as it had been in actuality, with both hatred and mortal terror. Just before his head disappeared he screamed, as he had not done that long-ago afternoon, "Murderess, murderess!"

I came awake sitting up in bed, drenched with sweat, hearing my own strangled scream. For a few seconds the river and Neil's face seemed to linger before my eyes. Then I felt Mike's arms around me. "Darling! What is it?"

I must have told him it was a dream, because he said, "It's gone now. Lie back down." Then: "Carla! You're shaking. What was that dream about?"

"Just a bad dream," I managed to say.

"But surely you can tell me about it. Believe me, it's the best way to dispel a nightmare."

But the nightmare arose out of a real event, one I could not tell him about. I think I could have told him almost anything else. If I once had been a shoplifter or check forger or a call girl, I could have told him about it. But I could not tell him that I had stood by, not lifting a finger, at least not until it was too late, while my little girl's father . . .

It was because I knew I would never be able to tell Mike that I had resisted, until that weekend, my growing physical need for him. Lying there in that Vermont bedroom, I realized I should have gone on resisting him. My guilt would not allow me to be happy with him, or perhaps with any man.

"Come on, darling," he had said, hand stroking my hair. "Tell me."

"Stop asking that! Stop—"

I did not say, stop tormenting me, but he must have known what I meant, because after a moment he said in a too-quiet voice, "All right. Try to sleep now."

The next morning neither of us mentioned my nightmare, but Mike's manner was restrained. It remained so as he drove me back to New York. We collected my daughter from Dodie Sims, and then Mike let Melissa and me off at our apartment.

That had been ten days ago. Twice since then he had telephoned. Knowing I should refuse, and yet loving him too much to stay away from him, I had accepted his dinner invitations. But it wasn't until now that he had suggested another weekend.

I said into the phone, "Mike, I'm too afraid—"

I broke off. After a moment he said, "Afraid of what? Carla, there's something important that you're not telling me, isn't there?"

I remained wretchedly silent.

"I love you, Carla." His voice was almost stern.

"I think I want to marry you. In fact, I know I do. But from the night we met I've felt you've been evading me in some essential way. And that's got to stop. I've talked to you freely about myself. Can't you be equally open with me?"

He certainly had talked about himself. His "kid marriage" to a college classmate, which ended when the girl discovered that she was not pregnant after all. The affairs since then, none of them of much importance. In return, I had talked freely enough of my childhood and growing-up years. But of Neil Baron I had said only that he belonged to the richest family in our part of Arizona, and that he had "drowned accidentally" in a river in the Azul Mountains, about fifty miles from Baronsville.

"Carla, I'm thirty-two. I want to settle down, preferably with you. But if you won't tell me what is standing between us—"

His voice trailed off. But his meaning had been clear. Before long he would turn to someone else. And heaven knew he would have no trouble attracting any number of young women. Just that thoroughly decent character of his would have been recommendation enough. But in addition he had an excellent job as a staff writer for *Nation's Week* magazine. And although he didn't resemble those sulky-looking males who model blue jeans, he was definitely handsome in a roughhewn way, with gray eyes under strong brow ridges that balanced a high-bridged nose, well-cut mouth, and a square jaw.

In fact, when I first realized that he was falling in love with me, a twenty-seven-year-old widow with

11

a six-year-old daughter, I'd felt a bewildered although delighted incredulity.

My voice sounded wretched even to my own ears. "I can't bring myself to tell you about it, not yet."

Several seconds passed. Then he said, "All right, Carla. I'll go up to Vermont alone this weekend. Perhaps I'll telephone you sometime next week, if that's okay."

Perhaps he would telephone. Only perhaps. I said wretchedly, "All right."

2

EVEN THOUGH I tried to attend to Melissa's chatter, Mike's words kept echoing in my mind as we ate our applesauce dessert. But after I had supervised her bath, and put her to bed, and shown her in the atlas where the Mediterranean was, and read to her a chapter of *Wind in the Willows,* and switched off her bedside lamp, I was able to turn to the best anodyne I know of for any sort of pain—work. At my Victorian-style desk in the living room, one of the several pieces I had added to the Witteralls' hand-me-down furniture during the past four years, I took a manuscript, designed for children aged six to eight, from my briefcase. I always found it easier to work at home rather than in my small office at Halstead and Sons, Publishers. Here the walls were so blessedly thick that my neighbor's TV set was only a murmur. Outside the circle of lamplight falling on my desk the room was soothingly dim except for the Kline print which I'd bought in a moment of reckless celebration when I was promoted to editor, and which seemed to glow with color—a cerise cube floating on a field of serene blue—as it hung on the wall a few feet from where I sat.

The manuscript began, "The Smith twins woke up one morning to find that their dog Prince was in a terrible fix." Nevertheless, I plowed on for a while, hoping that the story might contain possibilities which, with sufficient editorial help, would make the book publishable.

Just as I had been lucky in finding an apartment soon after I came to New York, I had been lucky in finding a job in a field I wanted to enter. In a city thronged with recently graduated English majors, I had feared I would not have much chance in publishing. True, I had been an English major, but I had left my small Arizona college in my junior year to marry Neil. The director of personnel at Halstead and Sons, though, had hired me as a clerk-typist, with the promise of a chance at a reader's job soon. Before long I learned that the personnel director, a divorcée, had raised three children by herself. Perhaps that was why, after I told her about Melissa, she was willing to overlook my lack of a diploma.

I typed and filed letters for six months and then was promoted to reader in the children's book department. The associate editor there and my immediate boss was Jim Allerdyce, an almost skeletally thin man past sixty. Soon I knew what everyone else did. Allerdyce performed almost no work at all. After glancing over manuscripts chosen by his assistant,

14

he would hand them on to the senior editor in that department and then, perhaps, go out for one of his two-and-a-half-hour, three–Bloody Mary lunches. Why the company tolerated him I'm not sure. Maybe it was because many years earlier he had helped snare a best-selling author for the firm. Maybe it was because retirement would rid them of him soon. Anyway, there he still was.

I had been a reader only a few weeks when, in a pile of unsolicited manuscripts, I found one written by a young couple in Detroit. Designed for six- to nine-year-olds, it was about, of all things, computers. As far as I knew, back then few or no writers of young children's books had used computers as a subject. I found the book not only instructive but good fun.

Since his assistant was on vacation, I took my find directly to Mr. Allerdyce.

"A book about computers? For six-year-olds? You must be out of your mind."

I argued with him for several minutes. Then I said, "I don't want to go over your head, Mr. Allerdyce, but I would like to know what Mr. Thornton thinks of this manuscript." Mr. Thornton was senior editor of children's books.

"Then ask him! But I warn you, you'll be making a fool of yourself. And there are hundreds of girls, hundreds of college graduates"—so he had looked up my personnel file—"who would love to have your place here."

That frightened me a little. But my faith in the manuscript was so strong that, late that afternoon,

15

I took it to the senior editor.

Halstead and Sons bought it. When it was published, it soared almost immediately to the top of the list of books recommended for children of that age group. Furthermore, it set a trend for young children's books throughout the industry.

As a reward, I was made an assistant editor in the young adult division, where there was an opening. And a few months later, when Mr. Thornton retired, I was made senior editor of children's books.

Jim Allerdyce really hadn't lost anything. Even if it hadn't been for me, the company would never have made him senior editor. But even so, my promotion over him must have been a shattering blow. I could have sympathized with him, had it not been for the hate visible in his face for a second or two whenever we ran into each other.

We kept those encounters to a minimum. Whatever manuscripts he passed along to me were brought to my desk by the pleasant young man who, nominally Jim Allerdyce's assistant, actually did all his work. On the rare occasions when I needed to communicate with Allerdyce, I sent a message by my own assistant, a girl named Hildegarde Owen.

Now, with a sigh, I laid aside the manuscript about the Smith twins and their dog Prince. After twenty pages, the writer still had not told me what "terrible fix" Prince was in. I dove into my briefcase for another sheaf of typescript. Like the one about Prince, it was an unsolicited manuscript. Every once in a while I took a pile of such scripts home with me, partly in hope of finding another gem like the computer book, partly as a spot check to see if publishable manuscripts were being passed over.

Soon the brass carriage clock on my desk, another purchase my promotion had enabled me to make, chimed eleven. I put everything back in my briefcase. My eyes burned, and my neck and a spot between my shoulders ached. But at least, pray heaven, I could fall asleep without thinking for too long of how much I loved Mike, and of the look that would come into his face if he ever learned the truth about me.

Even so, it must have been past midnight when I lost consciousness.

3

THE RINGING of my bedside phone brought me up through layers of sleep.

Few things are more alarming than the phone's ring in early-morning darkness. Lying chilled and rigid I thought, something must have happened to my mother. Or to my sister, Jennifer. Or to Chad Wilson, my stepfather. I reached out, lifted the phone from its cradle, and managed to say hello.

My dead husband said, "Come back to me, Carla."

As I had so often heard it, his voice was a little thick.

"Come back to me," he said again, "you and Melissa both. Everything will be different from now on. I swear it, darling."

There was a click.

For several moments I felt nothing at all. Then the incredulous horror hit me. Neil? Neil, who had been dead for four years?

Of course Neil hadn't called me. It was only in a

18

dream, another bad one, that I had picked up the phone and heard the voice of a man long since drowned. I reached out with my left hand and switched on the bedside lamp.

No dream. Or at least the part about picking up the phone had not been a dream. It was still in my right hand, just as real as the circle of light cast by the lamp, and the turned-back Indian print coverlet at the foot of my bed, and my blue flannel robe folded over a chairback.

Automatically I reached out and restored the phone to its cradle. A hallucination, then.

But hallucinations could mean insanity. And I mustn't be insane. What would happen to Melissa if I went insane?

Then could it be that Neil really had called me? Had he somehow survived that plunge over the falls into the boulder-strewn turbulence beyond?

Bathed in sweat, aware of the sick, faint beating of my heart, I stared at the ceiling and forced myself to relive that day more than four years in the past.

The day had started off well. In the kitchen of the two-story, ten-room guest "cottage" on his mother's estate, Neil and I packed a picnic lunch. At his suggestion, we planned to drive up to the Azul Mountains and to a favorite spot on the Azul River, where we would celebrate making up after our latest quarrel, an especially bad one which had lasted three days. Like most of our quarrels, it had started when I criticized his drinking. Now, spreading butter on whole wheat bread, Neil talked enthusiastically of how he was going to stop drinking and get a job.

19

"Hell, Carla, I'm twenty-eight," he said, in the tone of one who had just discovered that fact. "And it isn't as if I didn't have an engineering degree. Sure, I had only a C average, but a degree is a degree.

"And you and the baby and I ought to have a place of our own," he pointed out, just as if this were a brand new idea, rather than one I had pleaded for repeatedly. "We'd get along a lot better if we weren't living here right under my mother's nose, and under her thumb, too."

As often happened when he spoke of his mother, his voice was almost bitterly hostile. But I had long since perceived that it was more or less a false hostility. True, he resented her occasional bossiness. But the person he resented even more was himself, for being tied to her, dependent upon her.

We left Melissa with Mrs. Baron, who as always welcomed having her granddaughter all to herself. Then Neil drove our red Porsche between stone gateposts. Turning left, we passed several miles of the irrigated alfalfa fields Martha Baron had inherited from her husband, fields so profitable that locally their product was called "green gold." Then we were out on the desert, flat and tawny and dotted here and there with greasewood and with the grotesque, many-armed saguaro cactus. The car's top was down, and hot desert wind blew against our faces. But fifty miles away through the clear Arizona air rose the Azul Mountains, a deeper blue against the cloudless sky, those lovely mountains with their cool, pine-scented air and with the roaring Azul River.

Perhaps it was because I was raised in a town set

in southern Arizona's sandy wastes that I have always loved water. As a young child I learned to swim in the quieter stretches of the Azul River. In college I became a member of a women's swimming team which competed successfully against colleges throughout the Southwest.

We had gone only a few miles when he stopped at the roadside, reached across me to the glove compartment, and took out a flat pint of bourbon. When I cried, "Neil!" in disappointment and foreboding, he winked at me.

"Just a quick one, honey, to set the mood. After all, this is a celebration." He drank deeply, restored the bottle to the glove compartment, and drove on.

That was the first of several stops. By the time we reached our picnic spot on the riverbank a hundred feet or so above the falls, Neil was thoroughly drunk.

Angry and near tears, I spread a blue-and-white checked tablecloth on the needle-strewn ground and unpacked our ham and chicken sandwiches and fruit and cookies. Still genial, but intent on finishing the inch or so left in the bottle, Neil didn't even pretend to eat.

I don't know just when his geniality turned to shouting rage. But I do remember about what—or rather, whom—he shouted. It was Ben Solway, a former boyfriend of mine. Neil didn't like the way I had spoken to Ben, or smiled at him, the last time we had driven into the garage the Solway family owned.

"Don't tell me you haven't been sneaking into

town to crawl into bed with him! I saw the way you two looked at each other!"

Furious and bitterly disappointed, I didn't even try to refute the absurd accusation.

Suddenly he leaned across the checked cloth and slapped me, hard. He got unsteadily to his feet. Ears ringing, vision blurred, I looked up at him as he shouted, "Tramp! Filthy little tramp! I should have known better than to marry a girl from the wrong side of the tracks."

He spoke metaphorically, of course. No railway ever ran through Baronsville, although an unused, rusting spur still led from the Southern Pacific's tracks to what was once the Baron Copper Mines.

It was not the first time he had struck me. Once he also had laid hands on Melissa, shaking her tiny shoulders because her wails had awakened him from an afternoon nap. But he had done that only once. Somehow I must have convinced him that if he did that again I would take Melissa and leave him, permanently.

Now he was the one who talked of leaving. "I can't stand the sight of you!" he shouted. "I'm leaving, right now!"

He turned. I expected him to run to the car, and already I was thinking about what would be best to do if he managed to drive away, leaving me stranded up here. But he moved unsteadily, not toward the Porsche, but the water's edge. I saw him leap from the bank to the first of a staggered line of boulders in the seething water. He tottered there for an instant, leaped to a second boulder.

22

I was on my feet now. "Neil! Come back!" I ran to the water's edge.

Another leap carried him to a third jagged boulder. He had reached a point in the river now where the water ran deep and very swift. I looked wildly around me. The dead branch of a pine lay a few feet away. If he fell in, perhaps I could wade into the water, holding the pine branch, and extend it toward him. . . .

And then he had fallen in. The sound of the rapids and the roar of the falls downstream was so loud that I did not hear the splash of his falling, but I could see him out there, arms flailing the water, face turned toward me as the current swept him forward. Through the rushing sound of the water I could hear him calling, "Carla!" But even in his terror the face he turned toward me still held rage and loathing.

For a few fateful seconds I stood motionless, somehow paralyzed by the thought of all the times he had screamed at me, hit me, and that one time he had grasped our daughter's fragile shoulders. Then the paralysis dropped from me. I snatched up the pine branch and waded into the water, only dimly aware of its iciness biting through my blue jeans. I screamed, "Neil! Neil!" and extended the branch as far as I could.

But he was several yards beyond its reach now, dark head bobbing in the water, arms flailing. His face no longer was turned shoreward. Instead, he faced the spot where the river, no longer frothing and boulder strewn, but glassily, sinisterly smooth, brimmed over the lip of the falls to the even swifter torrent and more numerous boulders below.

I saw him go over.

For a moment I stood there, thigh-deep in the water, pine branch still in my hand. Then I was able to move. Letting the river take the pine branch, I floundered ashore. I ran along the riverbank, halted where the falls thundered down onto the jagged black boulders, almost obscured by high-flying spume, which toothed the river bed. There was no sign of Neil.

I have only dim memories of my drive down the winding mountain road and back across the flat desert floor. I did not stop at Martha Baron's house but drove straight into Baronsville and spilled out my hysterical story to the chief of police. I simply could not be the first to tell Martha Baron because I knew that, underneath her cold exterior, she loved her son fiercely, the way mothers do love a child flawed in body or mind or character, simply because he is flawed.

During the next few days the river was dragged to a distance of several miles below the falls. The fact that Neil's body was not recovered surprised no one. The bodies of some who had drowned in that river had never been found. Others had been recovered only years later. When I was a small child, there were weeks of abnormally low water along the Azul one summer. Some children, wading at the edge of the shrunken river in water which normally would have been far over their heads, found the partially disjointed skeleton of a man wedged under a boulder. His dental work, as well as an initialed

24

watch found at the site, identified him as a trout fisherman who, twenty years earlier, had been seen struggling in the river's grasp.

Two weeks passed before Neil's mother, giving up hope, arranged for a memorial service in the Baronsville Community Church.

But on that hot September day when almost everyone in town had tried to crowd into the church, was Neil in reality alive? Had he managed to escape the river?

But if so, where had he been all this time? And why should he suddenly call me in the middle of the night with a plea to "come back" to him?

His voice had sounded sincere, in a drunken sort of way. But he could not have been sincere. Otherwise he would have told me where to come to him.

No, his intent must have been to frighten me, torment me, reawaken in me all the almost unbearable guilt I had felt in the first days after he plunged over the falls.

I brought my thoughts up short. Somehow in the last few minutes I had almost convinced myself that Neil was alive and had telephoned me tonight. And that was impossible, or almost so. No, it was far more likely, sickening as the thought was, that the phone call had been a hallucination, induced by the memory that had seized me at the fruit and vegetable counter ten hours or more earlier. Either that, or it had been a trick someone played upon me, someone who had imitated Neil's voice, or hired someone else to do so.

But who here in New York had reason to dislike

me enough to do such a cruel thing to me? Jim Aller-dyce, perhaps. And perhaps Nicole Stacey, the tall blond model Mike had brought to the cocktail party where he and I had first met. Although I did not know it at the time, he had been taking Nicole out regularly for many months. He had escorted her home from the cocktail party, but I had every reason to think he had not taken her out since. Twice, though, Mike and I had run into her and her compa-nion, a man about three inches shorter than she was and with a married look about him, in East Side restaurants. Nicole's smile had been pleasant enough, but I had seen the flash of bitterness in her blue eyes at the sight of me.

Loving Mike as I did, I could understand her bit-terness. After all the preening male models she must have known, and straying married men, and self-satisfied chronic bachelors, Mike must have brought her the hope that at last she had attracted, in the popular Yiddish phrase, a real *mensch.*

But how could Jim Allerdyce or Nicole Stacey or anyone else here in New York know enough about my past to play such a trick upon me?

The answer was simple, of course. The Baron fam-ily was prominent enough in southern Arizona that stories about Neil's drowning and the search for his body had appeared, not only in the *Baronsville Weekly Post,* but in Tucson and Phoenix newspapers also. (I still felt a wave of guilt and resentment when-ever I recalled a sentence from one of those news stories: "Neil Baron's wife, the former Carla Jackson, who in college was a swimming champion, witnessed her husband's drowning from the spot on the river-bank where she stood.") Even without going out to Arizona, it would not have been too hard for someone to obtain photostatic copies of those newspaper articles.

But what if someone in Baronsville had been responsible for that call? A picture of Martha Baron's face at the memorial service rose before my mind's eye. I knew what grief must have been hidden behind that composed-as-marble face of hers. Mingled with it, I knew, was bitterness against the daughter-in-law who might just possibly have saved her son if she had acted more promptly. But I found it impossible to think of Martha Baron stooping to such a sly and cowardly, as well as belated, revenge upon me.

The faces of others who had been in the church that day flashed through my mind. My mother's face, filled with that dreary but unsurprised look with which she always had greeted each new disaster in life. My stepfather, Chad Wilson, looking unfamiliar and uneasy in his "best" suit, a navy blue that he almost never wore. My sister, Jennifer, her thin, plain face framed by the old-fashioned bonnet, shaped like a coal scuttle, which was worn by all the Protestant Sisters, an organization that maintained a mission for Arizona's impoverished and illness-ridden Apache Indians. Ben Solway, whom I might have married if, to my awed and foolish young delight, I hadn't caught the eye of the Baron family's handsome son and heir.

Ben had had reason to resent me, and probably

27

still did. And I could think of at least two others at that memorial service who might have had at least a slight grudge against me. There was a girl, two years older than myself, whom I had replaced on the college swimming team because my time for the Australian crawl had been faster by two-tenths of a second. And there was a man with whom my father, a year before his death, had become involved in a dispute over some carpenter's tools. With all the stubbornness that only the poor can bring to a dispute over what little property they have, my father had taken his fellow carpenter to small claims court in the county seat and won a judgment for eighty dollars.

There might be others in Baronsville with one grievance or another against me or my family. But the one person back there who might have a really strong motive to play such a cruel trick upon me was my cousin Mahlon. And he had not been at the memorial service. He had been in a state prison in Arizona, with five years left to serve of a ten-year sentence. It was reasonable to assume that he was still there.

And where could Mahlon or anyone else have found someone to imitate Neil's voice? Such an impersonation would require great skill. And the imitator would have to have known Neil well enough to recall that slight slur his voice took on after the first drink or two.

With sudden bleak certainty I thought, it was Neil on the phone. He hadn't drowned. He was out there somewhere, still filled with enough malevolence toward me to awaken me in the night with a mock-earnest plea to "come back" to him.

Terrifying as the thought was, I found it less so than the idea that I had hallucinated the whole thing. Because in that case the enemy which could destroy me, and leave Melissa parentless, was not out there in the night someplace, but inside my own brain.

The first dawn light was filtering through the Venetian blinds. You can still get about an hour's sleep, I told myself. You've got to. You can't let yourself go to pieces. You'll have to get up at seven-thirty, feed yourself and Melissa, get her to school, get yourself to work. Now sleep!

I didn't, of course. When the alarm went off I was still wide awake and too tense even to feel tired. Tiredness, I knew, would hit me later in the day.

4

IT DID. By late afternoon I knew what the phrase "leaden with weariness" meant. I had a sense that the blood circulating through my veins moved sluggishly, weighted with some metallic substance.

The crowded elevator in which I descended at five o'clock also carried Jim Allerdyce. Usually, unless speech between us was absolutely necessary, we acknowledged each other's presence with only the briefest of nods. But today, as I walked toward the lobby doors, he fell into step beside me.

"The job getting too much for you?" he asked. "If you don't mind my saying so, you look like death warmed over."

Too tired to even think of a response, I turned my head and looked into his bony face. He smiled, and then moved ahead of me to the revolving doors.

I picked Melissa up at her school. Unwilling to stand in line at the supermarket, I stopped on the way home at a small and very expensive market

30

on Park Avenue and bought a frozen packet of lamb and peas in cream sauce. Once I had fed us both, I put Melissa in her bed and crawled between the sheets of my own. Before I slid into blessed sleep, I had time to wonder if again the phone would shock me awake in the darkness.

It did not. I slept undisturbed until the alarm went off. There was no call the next night or the one after that. I started to swing back toward the belief that there had been no call, that it had all been a vivid dream or, at worst, a hallucination, one that, thank heaven, appeared unlikely to recur.

But when Mike called Friday night to suggest that we have dinner the next night, I was seized with the fear that he would somehow sense that something had happened to me in the interval since he had last called. And so I told him that I thought I was "coming down with something," and so had best spend the weekend at home.

On Monday night, or rather early Tuesday morning, the telephone's ring jerked me from deep sleep into almost instant consciousness. Sick with apprehension, I lay motionless for a moment. Then I sat up and switched on the lamp. If I was to hear that voice again, I did not want it to be in darkness. Midway of its fourth ring I lifted the phone from its cradle. Dimly aware that I held my breath, I waited for him to speak.

"Carla, honey, I know that I hit you." He paused long enough for me to remember his leaning across that spread picnic cloth to strike me with his open hand. "But it was only because I was drunk. And

31

I'm not going to drink anymore. Oh, I'm having a few tonight, but after this I go on the wagon. So come back, darling."

There was a click.

I sat rigid. Where was he? Somewhere in Arizona? Somewhere here in New York? I had a sense of him standing in a darkened room in the apartment building only a hundred feet or so from mine, binoculars raised to his eyes as he looked through the slats of the Venetian blinds to where I sat, phone still held to my ear, eyes fixed unseeingly on the wall.

I replaced the phone, switched off the light. Still sitting bolt upright I thought, the police. Let the police find out where he was, and why he was doing this to me. They could tap my phone, trace his calls . . .

And if, despite the tap, the police heard nothing the next time that voice called me in the middle of the night? Well, I thought bleakly, at least I would be sure then, sure that the voice came not from somewhere out in the darkness but from inside my own head. And, knowing that, I could seek psychiatric help, for Melissa's sake and my own.

I did not sleep the rest of the night. In the morning I took Melissa to her school and then phoned my office to say that I would not be in that day.

A little after ten o'clock I sat opposite a middle-aged plainclothesman, thin and baggy-eyed, in the Nineteenth Precinct stationhouse.

"Name?" His hand, holding a ballpoint pen, hovered over a pad of lined paper.

"Carla Baron."

"Miss, Mrs., or Ms.?"

"I use Mrs. You see, I have this little girl, and she goes to a Catholic school." I realized that nervousness was making me chatter, but I could not stop myself. "I felt that the nuns might think it —odd if I called myself anything but Mrs., and so I—"

"Yeah. What's the trouble, Mrs. Baron?"

I tried to speak more composedly. "Twice I've been awakened by a phone call in the early morning hours."

"Obscene calls?"

"No."

"Did this guy—I assume it was a man."

I nodded.

"Did he threaten you?"

"No, no!"

"You mean he's what we call a breather?"

"No! It wasn't like that! But it has to stop! You have to find him—"

"Look, Mrs. Baron, the easiest way to stop telephone harassment is to hang up on the guy, every time he calls. He'll soon get tired of his little game if you don't play. That's what it tells you right in the front pages of your phone book. Why ask someone to go to all the trouble of trying to find out who he is?"

There was no help for it. I would have to tell him the whole thing. "I already know who he is, or at least I'm almost sure I do. He's my husband."

Apparently it is true that the police dislike being involved in domestic troubles. Even though he didn't

33

actually move, I had the impression that he had shoved his chair an inch or two backward. "No matter who he is, if you don't want his calls, keep hanging up on him."

I clenched my hands in my lap. "You don't understand. My husband drowned four years ago. Or at least I thought—"

The change of expression in his eyes stopped me. He now had the look of a man long since grown weary of old ladies complaining that the neighbors had piped poison gas into their apartments, and old gentlemen convinced that their bridgework was being used by Russian spies to broadcast stolen military secrets back to Moscow.

"Why don't you put the whole thing out of your mind, Mrs. Baron? I'll bet you anything that'll work. And if it doesn't, if you still get calls like that, do what I say. Hang up."

Beneath my bewilderment and fear, resentment stirred. I said, trying to keep the angry tremble out of my voice, "Listen here, Lieutenant—" I glanced down at the nameplate on his desk. "I mean, Sergeant Biaggi. I'm a citizen and a taxpayer. I have a right to ask that this caller be traced."

A conciliatory note came into his voice. "I'm not disputing your right, Mrs. Baron. But you should have gone to the phone company. They'll trace calls, if you insist."

"I've heard the phone company doesn't like to go to that trouble. That's why I came to you first. They'll have to oblige the police."

His eyes seemed to say that perhaps I wasn't so

crazy after all. "All right," he said with a sigh. "Now what has this fellow, whoever he is, said to you?"

My stomach knotted with the memory. "Just that he loves me. Just that he wants me to bring Melissa, that's my little girl, and come back to him."

"Come back to him where?"

"He hasn't said, not yet, but I suppose he means the little town in Arizona where we both grew up."

"And what have you said to him?"

"Nothing. Even if I had been able to—to pull myself together enough to talk, I wouldn't have had the chance. Both times he hung up after he'd spoken only three or four sentences."

"If you want his next call traced, you'll have to keep him on the phone for several minutes. Talk to him, ask him questions."

Everything within me seemed to shrink at the thought of a conversation with that voice in the night. But I would have to keep him on the phone. Unless the owner of that voice was apprehended, I would have to run for it. I would have to quit my good job, take Melissa out of school, and move to some other city—only, perhaps, to have him find me again.

"I'll keep him talking," I said.

Sergeant Biaggi took down the basic facts—my address and phone number, and Neil's name. Less than an hour after I returned to my apartment, the phone rang. It was a man representing the telephone company.

"Sergeant Biaggi of the Nineteenth Precinct has contacted us. He informed us that you have been harassed by phone calls from a man who is, or pretends to be, your former husband." His voice was so impersonal that I could not tell whether or not Sergeant Biaggi also had informed him that in his opinion I might be crazy.

"We will monitor your calls from now on," the phone company man said. "If he calls again, we will try to find out where the call is coming from. But you must cooperate. Use the caller's name when you first speak to him, so that we will be sure we have the right man. And keep talking as long as possible."

"I will."

"If you want to consult us at any time, call our business office. My name is Hallowell, if you wish to ask for me."

"Thank you, Mr. Hallowell."

"You're welcome. It is all part of the phone company's service. Good-bye, Mrs. Baron."

For a blessedly long interval I had no need of that particular part of the phone company's service.

5

WEEKS PASSED. Bleak February gave way to an uncertain March, with dirty slush along the curbs alter-
nately melting and then freezing again. Among the
winter-pale pedestrians on Fifth Avenue, returnees
from Florida and the Caribbean began to appear,
swathed in mink and silver fox, but with faces still
copper-colored from the tropic sun. On milder days
toward the end of the month, buckets of daffodils
and tulips stood on benches outside florist shops. And
still the night caller left me in peace.

Sometimes I wondered if the phone company
monitored all of my phone conversations, including
the ones with Mike, and with the Puerto Rican
grandmother who baby-sat for me, and with various
people who called up to sell me dance lessons or
memberships in health clubs. I suppose those calls
were monitored. I wondered, too, if my tormentor
somehow knew that I had gone to the police, who
in turn had alerted the phone company. Perhaps

that was why he had left me alone.

The memory of the two times that slightly slurred voice had spoken to me in the early-morning hours began to fade. Sometimes several days would pass without my even thinking about those calls.

I still refused, though, to go away for the weekend with Mike. I was too afraid that if I permitted myself the bliss of going to sleep in his arms, my guilt would see to it that I woke screaming from another nightmare. But I did see Mike frequently, and several times we made love in his apartment. Those hours were good. They did not have the idyllic quality of that first night in Vermont, but they were good.

On a fairly warm night the first week in April, the phone's ring jerked me out of dreamless sleep into complete wakefulness.

After a frozen moment or two, I started to reach for the bedside lamp. Then, recalling how I had pictured him, binoculars in hand, standing at some darkened window nearby, I instead reached for the phone.

He said, "If you feel you have to stay away a little longer, I won't insist." Tonight he was drunk enough that the word came out sounding like *inshist*. "But I just had an idea, darling. When you do come back, don't come to the house. Let's meet up by the river. Remember how it used to be before we were married? Remember that night up there when we first made love? There was a full moon—"

My first paralysis left me. I remembered what to do. "Neil!" I cried. "Where are you calling from?"

He hung up.

So I'd blown it.

After a few seconds I replaced the phone. I got out of bed, crossed to the window, and adjusted the blinds so that no one could see in. Then I turned on the lamp. I did not have to look up the number I was supposed to call. I had written it, in large digits, on the cover of the Manhattan phone book I kept on the shelf of my bedside stand.

I dialed. After a couple of rings a voice said, "This is a recording. If you are receiving harassing or obscene phone calls . . ." The voice went through the whole thing, about how I was to hang up at the first obscene word, or if the caller did not respond the second time I said hello. "If you want further information, call this number between the hours of nine to five, Monday through Friday."

I hung up and looked at my alarm clock. It pointed to almost four-thirty. There was no use in even trying to sleep. Instead I lay in bed for a while, with a bleak resolution forming in my mind. Then I got up and dressed.

A little after nine that morning, from a lobby phone in the building which housed the company where I worked, I called the phone company business office. I asked for Mr. Hallowell, and seconds later he came on the line. Yes, he said, that call had been recorded, but there had been no time to trace the caller.

I thanked him and hung up.

Somehow I got through the morning. At noon I started walking toward a Madison Avenue restaurant, which never becomes too crowded until the more fashionable lunching hour of one o'clock. Midway of a block someone said, "Why, Carla! Hello!"

I stopped and looked at Nicole Stacey, the tall blonde Mike had dated regularly before I met him. She said, blue eyes bright with pleasure, voice filled with mock concern, "Why, what's the matter, dear? You don't look well at all."

"I've had flu. Nice to have seen you, Nicole." I walked on.

In the restaurant, eating food I scarcely tasted, I completed my plans. I would go back to Baronsville, just as that voice in the night had asked, and hope that there I could learn who my persecutor was. The hope was a slim one, I realized. Neil, or whoever was imitating him, could be anywhere in the United States—or in Canada or Mexico or Europe, for that matter. But it was the only hope I had. Certainly I could not go on like this, never knowing when I went to bed whether I would be able to sleep through the night or would be awakened by someone purporting to be the husband I had thought long since dead. Sooner or later I would break down, to the point where I could care for neither Melissa nor myself.

From a pay phone in the restaurant lobby, I called Mike's office. He was out to lunch, as I had known he would be. I left a message, breaking our date for that night, and saying that because of "family matters" I must make a trip to Baronsville, Arizona, right away. I also said that I would call him as soon as I got back.

After that I called my artist friend, Dodie Sims,

40

she of the riddles and the two Siamese cats, Flotsam and Jetsam. She would be delighted to have Melissa as a houseguest for two weeks, she said, and so would the cats. I could tell she meant it. I don't know how she does it, but I have seen Dodie work swiftly and expertly at her easel, all the time carrying on a long conversation with my voluble daughter.

In midafternoon I went to the office of the editor-in-chief, Phillip Cranston, a tall man with a shock of red hair and, so some people said, a temper to match. He had always been pleasant to me, though.

But he stopped being pleasant when I told him that I wanted to take my vacation immediately, starting the next day. "Absolutely not! The Carlton book has been promised for this week. Schimmerhorn promised her book for the middle of the month."

Joyce Carlton and Hannah Schimmerhorn were writers with whom I'd developed a close working relationship. "I must have time off," I said stubbornly, "to handle a family matter. Hildegarde can manage those books."

After a few more protests he said, "All right, you can go. But we've paid both those writers a hefty advance. If their books bomb . . ."

He didn't finish the threat to fire me, but it would not have mattered if he had. Much as I loved my job, I had been prepared to resign if he refused my request.

I spent the rest of the afternoon discussing with Hildegarde the work I was to leave in her hands, including the final editing of a book for ages twelve and up on hang-gliders, jacket copy for a preschoolers' book on farm animals, and a small mountain of correspondence. At five-thirty I picked Melissa up at her school.

During our brief walk home I did not tell her that I intended to fly to Arizona the next day. I dreaded telling her, even though I knew she would really not mind too much, not when she would be able to exchange riddles all day with Dodie, and at night share her bed with Flotsam and his sister, Jetsam, talented siblings who could retrieve crumpled-up paper balls tossed into the wastebasket. But I would have to tell her before dinner was over, because I intended to start packing my suitcase as soon as we had finished the meal.

The elevator let us off on the eighth floor. And there, standing beside my door, was Mike. As always at the sight of his tall body and roughhewn face, a little like that of a handsome Abraham Lincoln, my heartbeat quickened. Then I felt an impulse to burst into tired, nervous tears. I had so hoped to get away without having to parry his questions, at least face to face. It would have been a little easier over the phone.

Melissa shrieked, "Mike!" and ran toward him. He lifted her into his arms. "How's my big girl?" He kissed her cheek and then looked past her at me, face grim now, and saying nothing at all. Feeling doomed, I unlocked the door.

In the living room, he set my daughter on her feet. I said, "Go to your room, Melissa, and close the door." From her expression I knew that she had sensed the strain in the atmosphere and was curious enough about it to resist being banished, and so I added, "You can watch the rest of 'Little House on the Prairie' and then 'Buck Rogers.' "

She sped down the short inner hall to her room. Usually space operas before meals are strictly *verboten,* because they leave her too excited to eat. I heard her door close and then, seconds later, the boom of a sound track. Like most children, my daughter likes her TV loud. For once, I was glad of that.

Mike finally spoke to me. "You look like hell," he said, and I thought of how his ex-girlfriend a few hours ago had expressed the same opinion, although more delicately. "Now what's the idea of trying to sneak off?"

"I wasn't trying to sneak. I tried to phone you about it."

"Don't be childish, Carla. I know you knew I'd be out to lunch. Now why are you going to Arizona?"

"It's—confidential. A family matter."

"Confidential? From me?" He grasped my shoulders, none too gently. "Now talk straight. Why are you going out there?" When I didn't answer he asked, "Is someone in your family sick?"

"No."

Perhaps it sounds absurd, but I've always felt a superstitious reluctance to give the ill health of a loved one as a false excuse for anything, lest the lie become true.

His gray eyes studied my face for several moments. Then he said, "It's something about your husband, isn't it?"

I stiffened. How had he guessed that? Had I cried

Neil's name in the nightmare I'd had that time in Vermont? If so, Mike had not mentioned it the next day or at any time since.

Then my defenses collapsed. I could no longer keep hiding it from him—my guilt over Neil's death, those eerie phone calls in the middle of the night, any of it.

I said, aware of the dullness of my own voice, "I'll tell you. But I must sit down. I'm terribly tired."

We sat facing each other from opposite corners of the sofa. Mike waited. At last I was able to say, "You know that I saw my husband—drown."

Mike nodded. "You told me soon after we met."

"But what I didn't tell you," I said painfully, "is that I might have saved him."

I told all about it then. Neil's striking me, and then his drunken progress across the jagged boulders, and that paralysis that had held me for several vital seconds after he toppled into the seething water. "I ran along the bank to a point beside the falls, but by that time there was no sign of him."

I was trembling all over now. Mike drew me into his arms. "Oh, baby, baby! Why didn't you unload this on me a long time ago? There's no reason for you to feel guilty."

"But you're wrong! If I'd picked up that pine branch in time and moved far enough out into the stream—"

"If you'd tried to move through the sort of water you describe, you probably would have drowned too. Look, Carla. I can understand how you might feel guilty. You must have been hating him at that mo-

44

ment. He had been drunken, abusive, and finally violent. But I don't think even that could have caused you to withhold help from him deliberately. That would have taken a truly murderous hatred, and I don't think you're capable of it.

"It's a matter of reaction time, honey," he went on. "Only race drivers and tennis champions and a few people like that have split-second reactions. Just plain shock might have held you or almost anyone momentarily paralyzed."

I remained silent for a moment, taking at least some comfort from his words. Then I heard myself say, "But Neil thinks I wanted him to drown. That must be why he's tormenting me—"

I broke off.

Mike's hand, which had been stroking my hair as I leaned against his shoulder, became motionless. "Carla, do you realize what you just said?"

"Yes." I straightened up and looked him full in the face. "I don't think he drowned. I think he's alive someplace and taking his revenge on me."

Mike just waited. After a moment I began to tell him about the phone calls, and Sergeant Biaggi, and the telephone company. "Even after the second call I thought I might be having—hallucinations. But I wasn't! The phone company recorded that call last night. I mean, early this morning. You can call them if you don't believe me."

Mike took both my hands in his. "I believe you. What I don't believe is that Neil survived that plunge over those falls, and ever since has been hiding out somewhere. Someone has been playing tricks on you,

45

my darling, not your husband, but someone else. Hasn't that occurred to you?"

"Of course. But it sounded so much like Neil's voice."

"After more than four years, are you sure of just how his voice sounded? I don't think you can be. I think someone who knew him well enough to imitate him fairly accurately has been calling you. It also has to be someone who knew about his treatment of you just before he plunged into the river. Who could have known that?"

"Almost anyone in Baronsville," I said dully. "I remember telling the chief of police all about that picnic, for one, and I told my mother too. And that means the whole town knew."

The Baronsville police chief was an inveterate gossip. People said he held on to the job, not for the measly salary it paid, but because it enabled him to find out everyone's business. As for my mother, I suppose she found out long ago that talking freely of her troubles helped her to endure them.

"And that's why you're going back there?"

I nodded.

"Well, you're not going," he said flatly. His hands tightened around mine. "No matter who he is, the person making those calls is sick, and probably dangerous."

For a moment we were both silent. Then he said, "Marry me, Carla, right now. Afterward, if you like, the three of us can leave New York, or even the country. Remember my telling you that the magazine has made me a standing offer of a transfer to

46

the Paris bureau?"

"I remember."

"Living is pretty expensive there, but we could get by fine, especially if you held down a job too. Didn't you tell me you had two years of college French?"

"It wouldn't work," I said wearily. "He could still reach me from a telephone booth almost anyplace in the world."

I knew that was so. I'd looked up the information about international service in the phone book and seen that calls could be dialed to and from almost anywhere in the world, including Saudi Arabia, Yugoslavia, and Fiji.

"Carla, listen to me! Wherever we were, I'd be your husband, living with you, protecting you—"

"Don't you understand? I *can't* marry you, not if my husband is alive."

"Damn it all, Carla!" His voice was harsh. "Neil Baron's been dead for more than four years."

"I don't think so. He's alive."

I could almost feel him out there someplace. I didn't know how near or far, but he was out there.

Mike shifted ground. "All right. We'll talk about that again later. But if you're going to Arizona, I'm going with you. Postpone your trip until day after tomorrow. There are a few details I'll have to clean up at the office before I leave."

"No! I'm going tomorrow. I've made all the arrangements at the office and with Dodie Sims. And I'm going alone. I hope that Neil, or whoever is doing this to me, will decide to talk to me face to face.

47

And I don't think there would be much chance of that with you around."

"Carla, I've told you. This person almost certainly is dangerous—"

"And I've told *you*. If I don't find out who is responsible for those calls, I'm going to break down completely. And there's no 'almost certainly' about it. I'll go out of my mind."

We wrangled for another ten minutes or so. Dimly I was aware that in Melissa's room the theme music for "Little House" had given way to the shrill singing of Buck Rogers's ray gun.

At last Mike got to his feet. "All right." He sounded tired. "If you're determined to do this, I can't stop you. But keep in touch while you're out there. Will you do that?"

"Yes."

I stood up. He kissed me, held me for a moment in a tight embrace, and then started for the door.

"Mike."

He turned. "Yes?"

"That nightmare I had in Vermont. You guessed it was about Neil, didn't you?"

After a moment he nodded.

"How? I'd never told you in detail about the day he drowned, or about the sense of guilt his death had left me with . . ." My voice trailed off.

For several seconds he was silent. Then he said, "You called out something in sort of a strangled voice before you came fully awake. It sounded like 'knee,' but that made no sense, and so after a while I decided

48

you might have been trying to call out Neil Baron's name.

"Good-bye, darling." He added, "And for God's sake watch out for yourself."

6

LATER THAT evening I closed the packed suitcase on my bed and set it down on the floor.

The past few hours had been hectic. After dinner I had told Melissa that I was leaving. As I had anticipated, she demanded to go with me. Even after I explained to her that she was to stay with Dodie Sims and the cats, she still insisted it was unfair for me not to take her, when she had never been on "a 'nairplane." She had of course, but only when she was too young to remember it. However, even as she voiced her grievances, I could see by the gleam in her eye that the certain attractions of Flotsam and Jetsam had begun to outweigh the uncertain ones of airplanes and Arizona.

I packed a two-week supply of her clothing in a suitcase. I gave her a bath and put her to bed. I packed my own suitcase.

Now there was only one thing left to do before I took my exhausted self to bed. I had to telephone my sister, Jennifer, and let her know I was coming. I looked at my bedside clock. Ten-fifteen. Eight-fifteen in Arizona. The Apache children would have been fed in that austerely plain mission school in the Azul Mountain foothills. The older ones would have set the dining room and kitchen to rights. My sister would be in her small bedroom or even smaller adjoining office, perhaps reading or watching TV, but more likely writing still another letter soliciting funds for her always-impoverished school.

I sat down on the bed's edge, lifted the phone, and dialed. I did not have to look up the number. I called it frequently enough to know it by heart.

Jennifer and I were not real sisters. When she was still an infant, her own parents had been in an automobile accident which had killed them both and left Jennifer with a badly smashed right leg. Still childless after four years of marriage, Carl and Mary Jackson had adopted her. Five years later I was born.

Jennifer and I had our squabbles while we were growing up. But the squabbles were brief, and usually ended with me as the winner. I suppose it was partly because Jennifer was told by our parents that she must "give in to the baby." But I felt that even if we had been the same age, I almost always would have prevailed. Jennifer, I felt, was too gentle and generous in spirit to have insisted for long on her own way.

She remained crippled, of course. With her right leg several inches shorter than her left, her fastest gait was a lurching run. What's more, her face was plain, long-nosed, and too thin, with a pair of large hazel eyes as its only good feature.

But she was always popular with other children. When she was nine and ten—this I vaguely remember—she could hold neighborhood kids enthralled with stories she made up. Often they were stories about Apaches. Even as a child she must have felt a kind of kinship with the people who once had roamed and hunted freely over the land which now belonged to white men.

When she went on to high school she was still popular, although she couldn't dance or play basketball and hockey. I recall how often in the evenings her classmates would phone to ask her help with their math or Spanish or English homework. And I remember how impressed I was when she was taken into the Circle, a group of high school girls so elite socially that even we grammar school kids were impressed by them.

With the aid of a scholarship she went to Barnwell College, the state-supported institution I later attended. Upon graduating as a sociology major, she joined first the Protestant Sisters and then the staff of the Indian school in the foothills. Children from the nearby Apache reservation attended day classes there, and those who had lost their parents—to alcohol or disease or accident—were housed in dormitories. Now, at the age of thirty-two, she was the school's director.

Evidently she had been at her office desk, because she answered on the first ring.

"Jennifer, it's Carla. I just wanted to let you know that I'm flying out there tomorrow."

"Carla! How wonderful!" Then, in an altered tone: "Is something wrong? You sound—odd."

Better to let her know, right now. "I've been getting phone calls in the middle of the night."

"Phone calls?"

"They—they seem to be from Neil. Maybe he didn't drown, after all."

"Carla! How on earth can you—"

"Either it's Neil, or someone pretending to be him."

She was silent for several moments and then asked gently, "Have you talked to a doctor about this? I know how hard it must be for you in that city, holding down an important job, and raising a child all by yourself. Maybe you—"

"No, Jennifer." I tried to keep my voice calm. "I'm not having a nervous breakdown, not yet, anyway. Those calls are real. The last one was recorded by the phone company."

Again a silence. Then: "And you think that someone out here— Is that why you're coming out here?"

"Yes. I'm hoping he'll—approach me. Don't argue with me," I went on swiftly, "or I *will* go to pieces. And don't tell me to go to the police. I've been to them. What help can the police or the phone company give me when he hangs up before the call can be traced?"

"All right, Carla. I won't argue. You can stay here at the school."

"Thanks, dear. But I want to be in town." Inside the walls of that isolated mission school, I would be less accessible to the person I hoped would sooner

53

or later identify himself to me. "I'll stay with Mama and Chad."

She hesitated, and then said, "Carla, Mahlon's out."

"Mahlon! When?"

"He was paroled about four months ago. Mama and I agreed that there was no point in upsetting you by letting you know about it."

The news would not have upset me four months earlier. I knew that Mahlon was no good, but at least he wasn't a moron. Surely he had long since concluded that it was absurd to keep on blaming me for his imprisonment.

Or had he? Perhaps he still blamed me, to the point where he wanted to get even.

Apparently he had been free for some weeks before I received the first of those phone calls.

I asked, "Where is he now?"

"That's just it. He's staying with Mama and Chad. You know the way she's always been about Mahlon."

Yes, I knew. Perhaps it was because she had always wanted a son. (I think she named me Carla only because she'd been unable to name me Carl, after my father.) For whatever reason, she always had seemed to enjoy Mahlon's stays in our house.

Such stays had been frequent during my childhood. His mother, my mother's sister, had died when Mahlon was seven. His father, a traveling salesman who never stayed with any one employer for very long, sometimes took his son with him, and sometimes left him with us, the Jacksons, along with promises of board payments, promises that were more often broken than kept.

I said, "Even if Mahlon is staying with Mama and Chad, there'll still be a bedroom for me."

"All right, Carla. And no matter why you're coming, it will be wonderful to see you. I'll meet you at the Tucson airport, and you can tell me all about it on the way home."

"No, darling. I'll take the bus." I knew how little Jennifer was paid, and how much gasoline it would take for her to drive to meet me in her car, an ancient Ford with foot pedals especially adjusted for her handicap. "There's still a Tucson bus running through Baronsville, isn't there?"

"Of course. Things haven't changed that much in four years."

"Do Ben Solway and his father still run the garage next to the Baronsville bus station?" As I spoke I pictured Ben's curly, dark blond hair, square face, and warm grin—Ben, whom I might have married years ago if I'd had the good sense not to fall for Neil Baron.

"Ben runs it all by himself now. His father retired last year."

"Does he still have cars for rent?"

"As far as I know."

"I'll rent one as soon as I get there."

"I know you'll want to visit with Mama first. But drive out to the school as soon as you can, so that we can have a good long talk alone. I mean, much as I want to see my beautiful niece, couldn't you leave her with Mama until after we've had our talk?"

"She won't be with me, Jennifer. She's staying here in New York with a friend of mine who designs book jackets, tells riddles, and keeps cats."

"Oh, blast!" I've never heard anyone besides my sister use that expletive. Then, very soberly: "But I can see why you wouldn't want to bring her."

She paused. "You've told Mama you're coming?"

"No. You call her for me, Jennifer, please? I don't want to worry her with the truth of why I'm coming out there, and right now I'm too beat to think of another explanation. I'll think on the plane tomorrow. When you call her tonight just say I said I need a little rest."

"But she'll wonder why you didn't call her directly—"

"Say that I thought she might be out visiting the neighbors. Say I figured that if there was no one home but Chad, the call would be at least partly wasted. She'll accept that. You know how horrified she's always been by the cost of long-distance calls."

"I'll handle it. And Carla."

"Yes?"

"Be careful every step of the way."

"I will," I said, although I didn't see quite how I could guard myself against someone who so far had been only a voice in the night.

True, I was almost certain the voice had been Neil's. But even so, I might not recognize him if he approached me. For not the first time, I thought of what the jagged boulders below the falls, even if they hadn't killed him, might have done to that once superlatively handsome face.

I shoved the thought away. "Good night, Jennifer. See you soon," I said and hung up.

THE BUS that ran south from Tucson to the border was air-conditioned. Nevertheless, I knew that a wind—a hot, dry wind now that early spring was past—whipped the desert flats beyond the sealed windows. I could see the tiny whirlwinds called dust devils moving between the clumps of mesquite and the saguaro, those giant cacti which, with their up-flung arms, always made me think of Old Testament prophets, ranting at the multitude. In the distance I could see the Azul Mountains, indigo blue except in their shadowed folds, where they looked almost black.

A roadside sign said that Baronsville, the town named for Neil's family, was eight miles ahead.

Often I thought of how appropriate that family name was. Neil's people had lived—one almost might say ruled—like barons in this southwestern land for almost a century and a half. The first Baron, a younger son of a Virginia planter, had come out

57

here well before the Civil War. Some said that he'd had to leave Virginia because of a scandal involving extreme cruelty to a female slave. Whatever the truth or falsity of that story, he must have brought some money with him, because he bought a small, supposedly almost played-out silver mine. Through the discovery of another lode branching off from the one worked by the former owner, he made the mine more productive than ever. Later generations of Barons branched out into copper mining, then oil wells, and then, after a vast irrigation system was brought to the Southwest, cotton and alfalfa and oranges.

The Barons had married as shrewdly as they invested. The first Arizona Baron had gone back to Virginia to find a bride of suitable lineage. So had his son and grandson. But by the early twentieth century the family had enough branches that its members could find mates among their own second, third, and fourth cousins. Thus the Barons, priding themselves on their aristocratic bloodlines as well as their wealth, were able to look down upon the powerful families of Texas, say, who usually had nothing but money.

Neil broke the pattern. He married me, Carla Jackson.

Not that my people—the Jacksons and Townsends and Woods—hadn't been around here for a long time too. For more than a hundred years ancestors of mine had driven cattle in Arizona, and worked in the mines, and as craftsmen. My grandfather and my father both had been carpenters. Like Joseph, that most famous of carpenters, they also were poor men.

Not that I realized, as a child, that we were poor. I accepted our gray frame house and its sagging fence, just as I accepted my parents. No, I more than accepted them. I was proud of them. To me, my father was a man who could do anything he chose to do. And my mother was the source of everything good in the world, from cookies to hugs to medicine for my sore throat.

It was not until after I entered my teens that I began to realize that my mother's grammar was shaky and that she could be embarrassingly ignorant. She was capable of asking, right in front of my friends, "What's a Bee Gee?"

(Before I'd left Melissa at Dodie's apartment that morning, she'd thrown her arms around my neck and said passionately, "I've got the prettiest mama in the whole world." Now I wondered how many years would pass before she would begin to say, eyes rolled heavenward in despair, "Oh, Moth-*er*!")

As a teenager I also became aware that our house was neglected. During the rare rainfalls, there was always at least one leaky spot in the roof. Doors did not close properly, and the porch steps sagged. It was like the cobbler's children going barefoot. When not working on other people's property, my father went fishing in the Azul Mountains.

Nevertheless, I suppose my high school years passed as happily as those of most girls. I was popular enough. True, I was not invited to join the Circle. But then, I didn't help the Circle girls with their homework. If I was to have any hope of getting a college scholarship, I had to concentrate on my own homework.

Unlike Jennifer, I did not win a scholarship. What was more, my father died a week after I was graduated from high school, and for a while, between grief for him and concern for my mother, I thought I wouldn't be able to manage college at all. But my mother said that what with my father's insurance, and the job she had been offered at the Baronsville Department Store, she would get by. I too got a job, a part-time one, through the college employment office, and enrolled as an English major.

Ben Solway, a graduate of a business college in Tucson and a partner in his father's Baronsville garage, was my most frequent date during my summer vacations. I think that everyone, including Ben and myself, thought that eventually we would marry.

But toward the end of my junior year I met Neil Baron.

(Near the front of the bus a woman with coarse dark hair and almost expressionless black eyes had turned to look at me. After a moment I recognized her. Her name was Mary or Molly or something like that, and she was one of Martha Baron's several Indian housemaids. Often she had vacuumed rugs and mopped floors in the luxurious "guest cottage" which had been home to Neil and me during our married life. Smiling, I nodded at Mary, or Molly, and she smiled in return, or at least came as near to smiling as an Apache ever does.)

I met Neil when he and two friends of his crashed

60

the Barnwell College junior prom. They didn't belong at the dance or even on the campus. Neil had been graduated from Princeton four years earlier. His companions, I later learned, were distant cousins of his who also had attended Ivy League colleges. But there they were, tuxedo-clad, just inside the doorway. And none of the faculty chaperones was about to order them away, not when it was Martha Baron's money that had built the very gymnasium where the dance was being held.

Heartbeat quickening, I saw that Neil Baron's gaze was fixed on me. After a few moments he made his way through the dancers and tapped my partner—not Ben, someone whose name and face I've forgotten—on the shoulder.

Touch dancing for slow numbers had come back into fashion, bringing conversation along with it. He asked my name.

"Carla Jackson."

He not only smelled of liquor. His face had that blurred look that comes after too many drinks. And yet how handsome he was with a lock of dark hair falling over his forehead, and his classically cut features, and his mouth with the sensually full lower lip.

"My name's Neil Baron."

It was almost as if Robert Redford had said, "My name's Robert Redford." For at least six years I had been acutely aware of Neil Baron and had gazed after him whenever I had seen him driving through Baronsville in a blue MG or, later on, a red Porsche.

He added, "I'm sure I've seen you before, maybe

61

more than once. Where do you live?"

"Baronsville." After a moment I asked, "You've been at some other party, haven't you?"

"Connie Lipscom's debut." The Lipscoms, I knew, were rich cattle ranchers. "Strictly from dullsville. Not a girl there could hold a candle to you. Let's split and get a drink. The Half Moon's just down the road."

The Half Moon was a tavern of less than spotless reputation. "I can't walk out on my date. Besides, don't you think you've had enough?"

To my surprise he said, "I've had too much. I often do." He looked at me unsmilingly. "Maybe if I had the right kind of girl, I wouldn't do that."

I know. That's a line almost every lush in the world uses. But I was young enough, just barely out of my teens, to believe him.

Ben Solway cut in then, a proprietary glint in his eyes. When I again looked around, Neil and his friends had gone.

My first week at home that summer, I told my mother about the incident. "Don't go getting any notions," she said sharply. "Anyway, he probably was too drunk to even remember your name. Be glad of it. You've got a fine young man. Hang on to him."

A few days later Neil phoned and asked me to go to dinner at Markey's, a restaurant out on the highway with a largely upper-class clientele.

Pulse racing, I accepted, hung up, and turned to see my mother watching me with worried eyes.

"Don't go out with him, Carla. Call him back and say you forgot, but you've got another date. That kind, he'll just get all he can out of you, and then drop you flat."

My mother uses euphemisms like "get all he can out of you."

I said, "Mother, I can take care of myself."

"He's no good, Carla. Why, he must be around twenty-five, and he doesn't even have a job. Oh, he's supposed to be an assistant to that old Mr. Farnsworth or whatever his name is. Anyway, that business manager of his mother's. But I can imagine just how hard Neil works at *that*."

She went on, "Mark my words, girl, if you're not careful, you'll lose Ben Solway. And for what? A man who'll never marry you."

Three months later, after I had dated a usually sober Neil perhaps a dozen times, we drove across the Mexican border and got married in Nogales.

The elopement had been entirely his idea. "Why do we need a wedding and all that jazz? Getting married in Nogales will be just as legal."

I knew that the real reason was that he was afraid of his mother. He wanted to present her with the fait accompli of our marriage, rather than trying to gain her approval ahead of time. But in my infatuated state that made no difference. Even his relationship with his mother would change, I told myself, after we were married.

When the ceremony was over I telephoned my mother, and Neil telephoned his, from a public phone in the Nogales city hall. My mother did not sound overjoyed. Despite all the money to which Neil was heir, obviously she would have preferred

63

that I marry Ben Solway. But at least she seemed relieved that her worst fear—the fear of her daughter left heartbroken, humiliated, and perhaps pregnant—had not been realized.

Neil told me, after he'd phoned his own mother, that she'd taken it "pretty well." He added, "My mother doesn't like to appear too emotional. She thinks it's ill-bred, or something."

Besides, I thought hopefully, Mrs. Baron not only knew that Neil had been seeing me. She also must have realized that he had been drinking much less. Surely that would count in my favor.

As we stepped from the Nogales city hall into the late-afternoon heat and glare, Neil said, "She wants to see us as soon as possible."

It was around nine o'clock when, stiff with apprehension, I walked with Neil into that huge mansion a few miles west of Baronsville. Almost as daunting as the tall, sixtyish woman who rose from a chair beside the library fireplace were the Baron ancestors, looking down at me from gilded frames that lined the paneled walls. But they would be my child's ancestors too, I told myself reassuringly. And I intended to have a child as soon as possible. It would be the best way to cement our marriage, and to encourage Neil to keep his resolve and to get a real job, rather than to continue the fiction that he was assisting old Mr. Farnsworth, the man who throughout Martha Baron's twenty years of widowhood had been in complete charge of her estate.

"Welcome, Carla." Her smile did little to warm her face between its two wings of graying dark hair.

She bent and kissed my cheek. "I wish you and Neil had decided upon a more conventional ceremony." She did not say, although I'm sure it was the case, that she wished he had decided upon another sort of bride. "But what's done is done."

She turned to Neil. "As soon as you telephoned I sent the maids over to get the guest cottage ready for you and Carla, just in case you want to stay there."

We not only spent our wedding night in that luxurious guest house. We lived there throughout our married life. Almost from the first, things went badly. Neil got drunk four nights out of five, and when he drank we quarreled. Melissa's birth helped somewhat, for a little while. But soon my preoccupation with her, and her crying on days when he had a morning-after headache, became the source of more dissension between us. Once I even went away, taking Melissa with me. But after a few days in the crowded Tucson apartment of a college friend of mine and her husband, I decided to go back and give my marriage another chance. But things grew no better between us.

Finally, there had been that picnic lunch up by the Azul River . . .

The bus driver called, "Baronsville!"

8

THE SMALL frame bus station stood at the eastern end of Main Street, next to Solway's Garage. About a half dozen of us left the bus. Mary, or Molly, no doubt bound for Martha Baron's big house, was among those who stayed on.

In the shadowy garage next door a tall man in blue coveralls, back turned, stood beside the upraised hood of a yellow station wagon. I said, "Ben?"

He turned around, a man now in his early thirties, with curly dark blond hair, blue eyes, the kind of big chin you see on football linemen, and, at the moment, a smear of grease on his left cheek. "Carla Jackson, of all people!"

I knew that Ben had been very much in love with me, and that therefore he must have been deeply hurt by my turning to Neil. Perhaps he had recovered entirely, though, because the smile he gave me held nothing but warmth.

66

"What are you doing back in this neck of the woods?"

"Oh, I thought I'd visit with my folks for a little while. How have you been?"

"Can't complain. I guess you can't either. At least you're looking great." He paused. "The baby okay?"

"She's fine, although not much of a baby any longer. I left her with a friend."

I didn't ask if he had married. In almost every letter my mother contrived to mention that he had not. Instead I asked, "Do you still rent out cars?"

"Sure thing. Want one?"

"For a couple of weeks, or as long as I'm here."

He laid a wrench down on a workbench and led me out to where, against a fence separating his property from that of Eddie's Diner next door, a blue station wagon and two dark green sedans stood.

I asked, "They're all in good running order?"

"Sure. Otherwise I wouldn't let you drive one of them. That Chevy handles real nice."

"All right. I'll take it."

As we walked back to the glass-enclosed station office to complete the transaction, he asked, in a casual tone, "You haven't gotten married again?"

"No." Then, to protect him against a rekindling of his interest in me: "At least not yet."

"You mean, you've got some guy in mind?"

It was an apt way of putting it. All through the flight to Tucson and the bus ride afterward, the thought of Mike's beloved face, so filled with angry concern when I'd last seen him, had hovered at the back of my mind.

67

"Yes, there's someone."

After a moment Ben said, "Well, all the same, maybe you'll let me take you out once or twice while you're here, just for old times' sake."

"I'd like that very much, Ben."

A few minutes later, when I approached the old gray frame house where I'd grown up, I saw that my stepfather, Chad Wilson, was painting the gray picket fence. Evidently, he recently had repainted the house too. At least someone had.

I parked the rented Chevy in the driveway. Chad placed his brush in a cardboard paint-mixing bucket and walked toward me, beaming. "Shur-r-r," he said, in his Barry Fitzgerald voice, "and it's happy I am to see you, macushla."

Chad does impersonations. He impersonates Flip Wilson ("The devil made me buy that dress!") and Gary Cooper ("Yup!") and Bogart, complete with facial tic at the corner of his mouth ("Of all the cheap gin mills in the whole world, you have to walk into mine."). At any gathering where there is a piano, he plays and sings "Dig-digga-doo," pausing now and then to shake his head and say, "I got a million of 'em!"

At such times my mother is apt to remark offhandedly to whomever sits next to her, "I guess Chad's always been talented. He used to be in the movies, you know."

He was, sort of. Back in the days when small Hollywood studios ground out westerns at the rate of a dozen a year or more, Chad had been one of that group of extras known as the Gower Gulch Cowboys,

68

because of the bar on Gower Street in Hollywood where they gathered. Later he had done comic bit roles, specializing in what movie people call pratfalls. Dressed as a waiter, say, and carrying a dish-laden tray across a freshly mopped floor, he would let his feet go out from under him and then skid on his backside toward the camera, still holding the tray high and with an astonished look on his face.

It was such a pratfall that, about fifteen years earlier when he was around fifty, ended his career. He injured his spine so badly that he couldn't even sit a horse, let alone do comic falls. The movie company, with a generosity rather rare in the picture business, did not haggle over compensation but gave him a pension, payable quarterly. After that he wandered around the country, usually by Greyhound Bus. It was on such a bus trip that he had met my mother, about a year after my marriage to Neil. She had been on her way to visit a cousin in Phoenix, and he had been on his way to no place in particular.

Theirs had been a highly successful marriage. His pension had enabled my mother to quit her job at the department store. And he actually enjoyed doing all those house-maintenance jobs that my carpenter-father had shunned.

I got out of the car. Chad kissed me, his thin, grizzled face rough against my cheek. Then he hauled my suitcase from the car's rear seat.

My mother came hurrying down the porch steps, a small, still-pretty woman with gray-brown hair permanented into little curls all over her head. We embraced and kissed.

69

"Oh, my baby! It's so good to see you."

"Jennifer phoned you I was coming?"

"Yes. She said you told her that you needed a rest."

So Jennifer had kept her promise to give her no hint about my real reason for coming out here. Nevertheless, my mother looked a little worried about something or other.

She said, "Chad, honey, take Carla's suitcase into the hall." Then to me: "I'll bet you'd like a nice hot cup of my coffee."

"I'd love it."

We walked past my suitcase and then on down the hall to the kitchen. The faucet which had dripped most of the time during my childhood and girlhood was silent now, and the often gaping screen on the back door was intact. When we sat at the kitchen table with its yellow plastic cloth, coffee cups in hand, my mother said, "I sure wish you'd been able to bring Melissa."

"I couldn't take her out of school, Mother."

"I know, I know." Then, her voice tightening: "I guess Jennifer told you that your cousin Mahlon is here."

"She told me."

"I don't mean he's right here at the moment. He took the bus to El Paso this morning to see about getting a job there. But he's staying here, sort of temporary like, until he can find steady work."

"That's all right. I don't suppose he still carries a grudge against me."

"Oh, no! He don't at all." When I was about fourteen I began to correct her grammar—what horrible little twerps girls that age can be—and since then she'd tried to remember to say "doesn't." But sometimes she slips. "I brought up the subject this morning, and Mahlon said that was all water under the bridge."

"Which room is he sleeping in? My old room?"

She nodded.

"Well, don't disturb him. I'll just take Jennifer's old room."

That worried look I'd noticed grew more pronounced. "Carla, that's kind of Chad's office now. He's got a lot of stuff spread out in there."

"Stuff?"

"Old movie stills and newspaper clippings and a filing cabinet and a typewriter. You see, he's writing a book, his memoirs." She pronounced the word carefully.

"What's he going to call it?"

"My Life in Hollywood."

I forbore to say that I thought that title had been used. After all, he could always change it to *Gower Gulch Wrangler,* or some such.

"Honey, I know Chad will get his stuff out of there. He's already offered. But Carla, I hate so to ask him to."

I realized something then. My mother's wasn't just one of those middle-aged marriages of convenience. She loved Chad, as she probably never had loved my father. To her Chad was glamour and romance. And besides all that, he could always make her laugh. My mother hadn't had much to laugh about until now. In addition to poverty and hard work, there

71

had been two miscarriages of much-desired male children, and the lameness of her adopted daughter, and my own disastrous marriage.

It was the sort of personal history which moves more fortunate people to smile and say, "Why, it sounds like a soap opera!" But believe me, it can happen, and when it does it isn't very funny.

I covered her hand with my own. "I wouldn't dream of interfering with Chad's book. I can sleep on the couch in the living room." At our house it's called a couch, not a sofa. "I used to often enough when we had a flock of relatives visiting us."

"Thank you, honey! Maybe as soon as Chad's finished with the chapter he's on now—he says it's a tough one—it won't bother him too much to move his stuff into our room."

She sighed. "If the Baronsville Hotel still rented out rooms, you could stay there. But they closed the upstairs three years ago. Practically no business. The only other place is the Bide-a-wee Motel, and of course you can't stay there."

Scarcely. The Bide-a-wee, an establishment three miles from Baronsville, was aptly named. Couples seldom did bide there for more than a very limited wee, like a couple of hours, say.

"Don't worry about it. The couch will be fine."

Mahlon had not returned by suppertime. When the meal was over we all three did the dishes, Chad washing swiftly and expertly—"I don't want you girls getting dishpan hands"—and my mother and I drying. We had almost finished when the phone rang out in the hall.

My mother went to answer it. "For you, Carla!" Then, in a lower voice, as we moved toward each other: "It's Martha Baron."

I picked up the phone. "Hello, Mrs. Baron." She had never suggested that I call her Mother Baron, and I was just as glad she had not.

"Hello, Carla. Molly Birdfoot tells me you got off at the station in Baronsville this afternoon." She paused. "You didn't bring my granddaughter with you?" Not Melissa. Not your daughter. My granddaughter.

"I didn't want her to miss school."

After a moment she said, "I suppose that is a consideration. But since it is a private school, I should think some member of the faculty would have offered to help her make up any work she might have missed."

What could I say? That I had left my little girl safely in New York because I had come out here in hopes of encountering face to face a man who had been calling me in the early morning hours? A perhaps dangerous man who pretended to be her son, and in fact might be?

I could not tell her that. I had no great liking for her. But I did not dislike her enough to give her the perhaps false hope that her adored son was still alive. And so I said nothing.

After a moment she went on, "Nevertheless, I would be pleased to have you stay in the guest cottage while you are here. I never really closed it after—after you left for New York. Various relations and friends have stayed there. It is fully livable. And of course you'll have much more room than at your mother's house."

Why was she making the offer? Because she had come to feel at least a little remorse over bitter things she had said to me during our last encounter? It was her accusations, as well as the stares and whispers of the townspeople, which had caused me to flee to New York, taking with me my daughter and the few thousand dollars left in the joint account that Neil and I had held in the Baronsville Savings Bank.

And why hadn't she closed the guest house permanently? Was it because at night she liked to look across the broad rear lawn, and see lights in those windows, and imagine that her son still lived there?

Unattractive as was the idea of sleeping on the living room couch—and the idea was unattractive indeed, especially when Mahlon might be walking through that room late at night—I disliked even more the thought of staying alone in that house where I had lived for three years with Neil.

Then realization struck me. I had come back out here in the hope that I could lure my tormentor, whether Neil or someone else, into the open. Whoever he was, he would be far more likely to approach me in that isolated spot than in my mother's fairly crowded house in the middle of town. "Thank you," I said. "When shall I come?"

"Why not tonight? It is still early. Come to the main house, and I will give you the keys."

When I returned to the kitchen my mother asked apprehensively, "What did she want?"

74

"She invited me to stay in her guest cottage. I said I would."

"Then we won't get to see you hardly at all!" my mother wailed.

"Now look here," my stepfather said. "Your mother told me she'd talked you into not sleeping in Jennifer's old room. But I can clear my stuff out and work somewhere else while you're here."

He added, in the tone of one who doesn't believe a word of what he's saying, "The book's probably going to turn out lousy, anyway."

"Chad, don't say that! And you'll both see plenty of me. I'll just sleep there and take all my meals here, starting with breakfast tomorrow. After all, it's only a few miles' drive."

9

ABOUT AN HOUR later I sat with Martha Baron in her portrait-hung library. The high-backed chairs in which we sat faced each other across the fireplace. Even though the evening was not in the least cool, a fire snapped in the hearth beneath the gray marble mantelpiece. Four years earlier Mrs. Baron would never have ordered a fire kindled except on the coldest nights of the brief southern Arizona winter. Perhaps, despite her erect posture and thinner but still handsome face, she had aged a lot during the last four years. More likely, it was brooding over the loss of her son that had thinned her body and slowed her blood, so that she needed the fire's comforting warmth.

She said, "I still wish you had brought my granddaughter with you."

Not for the first time I wondered why she had not tried, four years earlier, to gain custody of Melissa. Heaven knew she'd have had the money to

76

wage a legal battle through any number of courts. Perhaps then she had been too shattered by grief to contemplate such action. But surely since then she often must have wished that she had tried to keep me from taking my little girl to New York.

An uneasy thought assailed me. Could she be harboring, even at this late date, some notion of gaining her grandchild's custody? But all I said was, "I too wish I could have brought her, but she needs to stay in school. I don't want her to get the idea that school isn't important."

"Yes, I suppose you have a point there."

Her gaze went past me to a spot on the wall behind me. Without turning my head I knew that she was looking at a portrait of Neil—Neil at seven in white linen shorts and a blue blazer, seated in a big red leather chair with one sock-clad leg folded beneath him, and a look of supreme confidence on his handsome, little-rich-boy face.

Suddenly I wondered if she was remembering our last interview in this room, only minutes before a taxi had driven Melissa and me into town to catch the bus for Tucson and a New York–bound plane. She had said, in a coldly even voice, "I have instructed my lawyer to set up a substantial trust fund for my granddaughter, payable to her at the age of twenty-five. But I think it only fair to tell you that you can expect nothing from me, either now or later."

The news scarcely came as a shock. "Under the circumstances, I really couldn't expect you to leave me anything."

77

She had looked at me for several seconds. Then her composure had broken. "What I will never understand is how you, a strong young woman and an excellent swimmer, could just have stood there and let my poor boy . . ."

I said nothing. Over and over I had explained—to the chief of police, to Mrs. Baron, to the coroner at the inquest—that it was a kind of paralysis, not a deliberate decision to watch my husband drown, which had held me motionless for those fatal few seconds. But if by then I had not convinced Neil's mother of that, I never would be able to.

"And you even besmirched his memory," she had said. Her voice, usually so cool and dignified, had begun to shake. "I don't know why. Perhaps you hoped to justify yourself. But anyway, you told people that he had struck you. My son, whose ancestors were gentlemen long before this country was founded! And you tried to portray him as a wife beater."

No matter how she had tried to deceive herself, she must have known her son was exactly that. But I found I had no taste for arguing with this distraught, grieving woman. I had said good-bye and gone out to where Melissa and our luggage waited in a taxi.

Now she said, her gaze returning from Neil's childhood portrait to my face, "As I told you over the phone, I have kept the guest cottage completely livable. The phones are connected. So is the air conditioning, if you feel a need for it. Molly Birdfoot and her sister have placed food in the refrigerator and made up the southeast bedroom for you. I was sure you would not want to sleep in the master bedroom."

The one Neil and I had shared. "No, I wouldn't."

"I've left the master bedroom exactly as it was." Just the slightest tremor in her voice now. "My son's belongings are still in there."

She paused, and then went on, "I hope I don't have to explain why I have not offered you a room in the main house."

No, she didn't have to explain. Out of a sense of duty to her grandchild's mother, or perhaps some other reason, she had offered me the "cottage," that spacious structure built like the main house of white brick, and separated from it by a broad lawn. But she couldn't bear the thought of having me under the same roof with her.

"I understand." I got to my feet. "If you'll excuse me now, I'll drive my car back to the guest cottage."

When I had finished unpacking my suitcase I sat in a straight chair for a moment and looked around the southeast bedroom. With its fine mahogany furniture gleaming against pale pink walls, it was one of five bedrooms on the second floor, each with its own bath. Then, irresistibly drawn, I got to my feet and went down the broad mahogany staircase to the lower hall. Turning on lights as I went, I began to move through the luxurious house where I had spent three stormy years. First I went into the living room which, with its bright chintzes and Aubusson carpet and eighteenth-century-style furniture, looked like a room in an English country house, rather than one in the Arizona desert. The library across the hall, though, was definitely western, with Navajo rugs on the well-oiled oak floor and a black leather sofa and matching armchairs drawn up in front of a stone fireplace large enough for roasting a Texas longhorn. It was in this room that Neil and I, on our rare amicable evenings, had played Scrabble or watched TV. Beyond was the dining room, again definitely western in feeling, with a wrought-iron chandelier above a long, mission-style table.

The kitchen was next. There everything gleamed, from the floor of red inlaid linoleum to the long stainless-steel sink and all the appliances, including an infrared wall oven. After that I went down a short hallway with four small servant rooms opening off it, their narrow beds stripped and with mattresses rolled back. Those rooms had never been occupied during the years I lived in this house. The Indian nursemaid, her wages paid by Mrs. Baron, had shared an upstairs bedroom with Melissa. As for the housework, I did it, aided by the maids Mrs. Baron sent over two mornings each week.

Turning off lights now, I moved back to the broad entrance hall. In the utter stillness my footsteps sounded loud. I climbed the stairs and looked into two more of the bedrooms, each with its reading lamp above the head of the bed and satin comforter folded across the foot, each with a jar of potpourri on the dressing table. I looked into the bedroom where Melissa and the Navajo nursemaid had slept. Only the nurse's bed was still there. Melissa's small bed with its high-railed sides had been removed.

Finally I stood, hesitant, before the door of the

room I had shared with Neil for three years. I tried the doorknob. It didn't turn.

The guest cottage keys which Martha Baron had handed to me did not include the key to this door. But I was sure I knew where to find such a key. As I returned to the ground floor I had no sense that I was about to do something underhanded. I had come out to Arizona to try to find out who threatened my sanity if not actually my life. I felt justified in taking any course that might help me do so.

In the kitchen I descended well-lighted stairs to the playroom. Like the rest of the house, it was luxurious, paneled in lustrous oak and thickly carpeted in dark red wool except for a twelve-foot-by-twelve-foot dance floor. The decor, chosen by Neil, was Mexican. Striped serapes in bright colors adorned the walls. Next to the door that led into the rest of the basement he had hung a huge sombrero, banded with a string of silver coins. Beside the dance floor a large bass drum, flanked by two snare drums, bore a painting of a fiercely mustachioed Mexican bandit. Next to the drum set a guitar leaned against its stand.

Neil's expensive hi-fi equipment stretched across one wall. He had installed the system a few months after our marriage. He had won the money for it, he said, by placing a bet on the Super Bowl with a Las Vegas bookie. By that time I'd learned enough about him to guess that he had really gotten the money from his mother but was too ashamed—or too resentful of his dependence upon her—to admit it.

At the opposite end of the room was the bar, its

81

half dozen tall red leather stools lined up in front of it and a few partially filled bottles standing on the mirror-backed shelves behind it. I walked toward it, thinking of the parties we'd given down here in the early days of our marriage. Almost invariably they had ended with Neil accusing me of being too friendly with some male guest, and so finally we had ceased to give them.

At one end of the bar a door about one foot square was set in the paneled wall. I opened it. Inside a little cupboard more than a dozen keys, each of them tagged, hung from hooks. I took down the key labeled master bedroom. Upstairs, I hesitated for a moment before that familiar door, and then unlocked it and touched the wall switch.

Light from the ceiling chandelier poured down on the mahogany four-poster where sometimes I had made love with Neil, sometimes quarreled with him, sometimes lay wide awake while he slept heavily beside me. I walked over to his bureau where his silver-framed comb and silver-backed military brushes gleamed in the light. Beside them sat a brass box, a little larger than a cigar box and engraved with his grandfather's initials, in which he kept cuff links, neck chains, and other masculine jewelry. Just as it had always been except when Neil himself opened it, the box was locked, but I had no doubt that his mother had left its contents undisturbed.

Briefly I looked into the bureau drawers. Shirts and socks and underwear. I didn't bother to look into my bureau, its top bare of even a scarf. The night before Melissa and I boarded that New York–

bound plane, I had packed all the clothing I wanted to take with me and given the rest to Melissa's nursemaid.

I opened the sliding doors of the wide closet, stretching across one wall, which had served us both. Nothing of mine in there now, just Neil's slacks and sport jackets and tuxedos and several of the tan western-style suits he had liked, their lapels piped in dark brown. A long row of footgear—loafers and dress shoes and boots of various heights—were lined up against the wall.

Suddenly I remembered that I had left something on the shelf of this closet, a small white photograph album holding snapshots I had made of Melissa during the first few months of her life. She and I had already boarded the plane in Tucson before I realized, with dismay, that in my distraught state I had neglected to pack that album.

I stepped back into the room and looked up onto the shelf. Yes, something white up there. I carried my dressing table bench, its seat padded with blue quilted satin, over to the closet. After kicking off my shoes, I climbed up onto the bench.

The album was there, but as I started to reach for it I saw that the shelf held something else back in the corner, something that gleamed dully. Already sure of what it was, I grasped it and then stepped off the bench.

A small, flat gun. Despite having been raised in the Southwest, I had little acquaintance with guns and even less liking for them. But I did know enough to recognize this one as an automatic. Furthermore, thanks to TV, I knew how to pull out the clip. As nearly as I could tell, the gun was fully loaded with bullets of some small caliber, .22s probably. I shoved the clip back into place and then just stood, staring down at the ugly little thing on my palm.

When, I wondered, had Neil put that gun on the shelf? During his drunken rages against me, had he ever thought of using it? Perhaps he would have eventually, if it had not been for the way that "reconciliation picnic" up at the Azul River had ended.

Here in this warm room, the thought quite literally chilled my body. For the first time I really faced what could happen to me in this guest house, with the police more than four miles away, and with no one in the main house except women servants and a mistress who had no reason to like me.

I would keep this gun beside my bed tonight.

I placed the automatic in my skirt pocket. I climbed back onto the bench, took the album down from the shelf, and carried it to the southeast bedroom. Even though I had locked the front door after me when I entered the house, and then made sure that the back door also was locked, I had not checked the downstairs windows.

Now I did so. Aware of the gun in my pocket, I again moved through those downstairs rooms. Every window was locked. Once I had made sure of that I climbed to the southeast bedroom. I placed the gun in the drawer of the bedside stand, undressed. I left the light burning in the upstairs hall, even though I knew that Mrs. Baron, looking out her own window at the glow of light, might feel I was abusing

84

her hospitality. Like many rich people, she could be extravagantly generous with those she loved or with favorite charities, and yet wax indignant over a light left burning.

For a long time I lay awake, wondering if soon I would hear a sound outside one of those locked windows, wondering too if the extension phone on the stand beside the bed would ring, and my husband's voice would say, "Carla, honey . . ."

The house remained utterly still. Not even the ticking of the big standing clock in the lower hall carried to my ears. Finally I lost consciousness.

10

I SLEPT more than my usual eight hours. But because of the time difference between New York and Arizona, it was still only a little past six when sunlight streaming through the bedroom window awoke me.

Because I had promised to have breakfast with Mother and Chad, I prepared only a cup of coffee from the supplies Molly Birdfoot had stocked in the refrigerator. When I had finished it I looked at my watch. Seven-forty here, nine-forty in New York. At the phone in the downstairs hall I gave the operator Dodie's number and asked that the call be charged to my New York number. A minute or so later I was talking to Dodie. My daughter was fine, she said. She had taken her to school about an hour ago and would pick her up at three.

After that I called Mike at his office. He asked, "Are you all right?"

"Of course."

"Where are you staying? With your mother?"

"No, it's too crowded there." I hesitated. Best not to let him know I was staying alone in this guest house. "Mrs. Baron asked me to stay with her."

"Neil's mother?"

"Yes."

That seemed to trouble him. He was silent for a moment. Then: "Carla, give this up. Come back to New York."

"We've been through all that. I have to know the truth. And I'll never learn it in New York."

Again he was silent. Then he said, "You'll keep in touch?"

"Yes. I'll phone again soon." How could I keep from it? Just the sound of his voice had brought me at least a temporary sense of warmth and safety, as if he had put his arms around me.

I went to the rented Chevy and drove it down the drive, past the big white brick house. No sign of life there except a gardener who looked to be at least part Indian. He was piloting a riding mower over that velvety lawn which, in this arid climate, must have cost Martha Baron a fortune to maintain. I turned onto the road.

After four years in Manhattan, where on even the brightest days there is at least some haze in the air, I had forgotten what a southwestern morning could be like. A sky so deeply blue it almost made your eyes ache. The scent of sagebrush and creosote bush. And the Azul Mountains, looming so clear through the sparkling air that they looked, not fifty miles away, but five.

At my mother's house I came in the back way

87

and found her and Chad in the kitchen, she looking into the oven, he opening a jar of honey at the sink. As I walked into the room he turned toward me and sang, in a fairly creditable imitation of Nat King Cole's butter-smooth voice, "A pretty girl is like a melody."

I said, "I know! Bing Crosby!"

Aware that I was kidding, he grinned and said, "Hot biscuits and sage honey and your mother's bacon-and-cheese omelet for breakfast."

After the meal, which I hoped would not prove too disastrous to my figure, Chad went up to Jennifer's old room to work on his memoirs. Mother and I dawdled through a little housework and then sat on the back steps, shelling peas for lunch.

She said, "Arp is having its weekly bingo game in the church basement this afternoon." By Arp she meant the Association of Retired Persons. "Like to come with us?"

"If you don't mind, I think I should see Jennifer today."

"That's right, honey. Better phone ahead, so that she can arrange to be free this afternoon. You know how busy she is up there."

For about forty miles, the road that leads to the mission school is the same one that leads to the crest of the Azul Mountains. Even though I tried to keep my gaze straight ahead that afternoon, I was acutely aware of a certain notch in the mountains' silhouette. Less than two miles beyond that notch lay the spot on the riverbank from which I had watched Neil struggling in the water. I was glad when I reached the side road which led through the foothills.

I followed it over gently rising ground and then went through a pair of opened wooden gates in a tan adobe wall. Beyond rose the flat-topped, two-story mission school, built of the same tan adobe.

Before I'd even stopped the car Jennifer came out of the shadowy doorway and limped rapidly across the hard-packed earth, a smile on her bonnet-shadowed face.

We kissed. "Let's go up on the roof," she said. "It's nicer there."

Beyond the entrance lay a hall floored with roughly shaped brown tile. Two classrooms opened off it. In one room very young children, presided over by an Indian girl of about twenty, were reciting the alphabet in unison. In the second, older children watched another young Indian woman chalk a long-division problem on the blackboard. In each classroom a few children turned sleek, blue-black heads and looked at us from solemn dark eyes.

My sister and I climbed to the second floor, which held the children's dormitories as well as Jennifer's office and bedroom. Then we climbed another flight to the flat, sun-drenched roof. Two birch chairs of obviously Indian craftsmanship, the bark still clinging to the supple wood in places, faced each other across a battered pine table which probably had been someone's gift to the school.

"Take the bigger chair," Jennifer said. "It's more comfortable." I noticed how, with her usual tact, she had placed that chair with its back to the mountains.

She sat down opposite me, took off her bonnet, and turned her face, hazel eyes closed, up to the warm sunlight for a moment. Then she said, smiling at me, "How does it feel, after seven years, to wake up on the maternal couch?"

After a startled moment I realized that it indeed had been seven years, three of them spent with Neil and four in New York, since I had slept beneath my mother's roof.

"I'm not staying there. Mrs. Baron offered me the use of the guest cottage."

I saw surprise in her face, and then something almost like consternation. "You're staying alone there?"

I nodded.

"You mean, you don't even have one of the maids sleeping there?"

"No. Mrs. Baron didn't even suggest it."

"But, Carla! It may be dangerous for you to stay alone there."

"I didn't come out here to be safe. I came out here to try to find out who's trying to drive me out of my mind. And I think I'll have a better chance of that sleeping in the guest cottage than on Mama's living room couch."

After a moment she sighed. "I don't suppose there is any point in my arguing. You always were a stubborn little thing. But I still think it's too dangerous. . . ."

Her voice trailed off. Then, with an association of ideas I found easy to follow: "Have you seen Mah-

90

lon since you've been here?"

"Not yet. But I don't think he could have had anything to do with those phone calls. Maybe I'm wrong, but I feel he isn't bright enough to manage something like that. Besides, Mama says he no longer holds a grudge against me."

"Well, perhaps he doesn't." She paused. "Speaking of phone calls, when you called me from New York night before last you said nothing about Mike Trenton. Are you still crazy about him?"

"More than ever. And he wants to marry me, Jennifer. That's another reason I must know the truth. If Neil by some miracle is still alive . . ."

I stared down at my clenched hands. After a moment she said softly, "Poor baby."

So Jennifer Jackson, thirty-two, almost certainly a virgin and almost certain to remain one, could express compassion for *me*. That didn't surprise me. She had always been like that. But it did impress me.

I looked at her thin, sun-browned face, at her brown braids pinned around her head. A few gray hairs gleamed in the bright sunlight. But otherwise she had changed scarcely at all in the four years since I had seen her. Come to think of it, she hadn't changed much in several years before that. Could it be, I wondered, that her face remained so little changed because nothing much happened to her, just the way a page remains blank if nobody writes on it?

I blurted out, "How are you, Jennifer, really?"

"Why, I'm fine. What else should I be?"

"But don't you ever get lonely, up here in these hills?"

"Lonely, with seventeen children here all around the clock, plus two teachers and a cook in the daytime?" After a moment she added, "Or did you mean lonely for a man?"

I floundered, "Why, no, not exactly. I mean, I know you find your work rewarding. But I have sometimes wondered if there had ever been anyone—"

I broke off, dismayed. There *had* been a man in my sister's life, I remembered now, back when I was fifteen and she was in her junior year of college. He'd come to dinner at our house several times during her summer vacation, a pleasant young man who recently had received his Doctor of Divinity degree from a Baptist seminary in Tucson. My mother had entertained great hopes. But the young man, called to a church in Louisiana, eventually wrote to say that he was engaged to one of his parishioners.

"Yes," Jennifer said, "there was a man once. I was crazy about him, but he preferred someone else."

She went on, smiling now, "I know how my life must seem to you, but that's only because you're pretty and have that glamour job in New York and so on. But if you look at it from another angle, you'll see how lucky I am. I could have been killed in that accident that killed my parents, but I wasn't. Or I could have come out of that smashup badly disfigured, or minus a leg. Instead all I've got is a limp. I could have been born with a low IQ. Instead I have a pretty good one. And I like my work here."

Her voice became teasing. "Just think, I've got seventeen children. Do you think you'll ever have seventeen children?"

I laughed. "I should hope not!"

"Besides," she went on, in a tone of quiet pride, "it's nice to be appreciated, and people do seem to appreciate what I've been doing here."

That was an understatement. Several years ago the governor of Arizona, acting on behalf of the Society of Friends, had given her a medal for her work at the mission school. After that she had become something of a public figure, appearing on talk shows presented by local TV stations throughout the southern part of the state.

I said, "You certainly are appreciated. In fact, I guess you'll remain the only celebrity this family's ever had—unless, of course, Chad's book wins the Pulitzer."

We both laughed. Then for a while we reminisced. About Howard, a more-or-less bloodhound we'd once had who, when we tried to evict him from the house to his bed under the back porch, would pretend to be dying, his breath labored and his eyes rolled piteously upward. We talked, too, of the time when I was five and Jennifer almost eleven, and we had wandered away from a desert barbecue attended by our parents and their friends. I had slipped going down a gully's side and landed in a patch of prickly pear. Too embarrassed to let the adults know of my predicament—some surely would have laughed—I howled down Jennifer's attempts to lead me back to the barbecue. She'd had to lay me across her lap and, using her thumbnail and a sharp-edged stone as tweezers, extract at least a dozen spines from my small bottom.

It wasn't until I was about to leave that Jennifer again referred to my stay in Martha Baron's cottage. "Do you make sure at night that the doors and windows are locked?"

"The ground-floor windows, anyway. There are no trees around the house. Anyone hoping to get in the second-floor windows would have to have wings."

"Or an extension ladder."

"Remember the squealing noise those extension ladders of Dad's used to make when he pulled them out to their full length? And they always thumped when he leaned them against a wall. If someone tried that at the guest house I'd have slammed the window shut and phoned for the police before he even started up. Either that, or I'd wait beside the window until he was three-fourths of the way up and then push the ladder over."

She sighed and shook her head, as if saying she'd always found it tough to win arguments with me. We kissed and said good-bye, and then I drove back to Baronsville through the bronze light of late afternoon.

11

I ENTERED my mother's house through the back door. To my call, "Anybody home?" there was no response. Evidently they were still playing bingo.

The phone rang, and I went down the hall to answer it. It was Ben Solway. "You said you'd let me take you out while you're here," he reminded me. "Would you like to go to dinner at the hotel tomorrow night?"

Even though the hotel had closed its upstairs rooms, it still rented out its lobby for meetings of the Elks and similar groups, and still served meals in its dining room. In fact, it offered the best food in town, although that wasn't saying much.

"Thank you, Ben. I'd like that."

"Then I'll pick you up there at seven."

"Ben, I'm not staying here at my mother's. I'm staying in Martha Baron's guest house."

There was a disconcerted silence at the other end of the line. I could understand it. Anyone who knew how bitterly Mrs. Baron had felt toward me would be surprised that she had offered me any sort of hospitality. In fact, I had been surprised by it.

"All right. I'll pick you up out there."

"Better not." Mrs. Baron would take an understandably dim view of my admitting a former boyfriend to the house she had provided to her son and me during our marriage. "I'll drive in and meet you at the hotel."

"Whatever you say. See you at seven."

I hung up and walked back to the kitchen.

A man stood leaning against the sink board. Because his back was to the sunset light coming through the window above the sink, it took me a moment to realize he was my cousin Mahlon.

Involuntarily my gaze shifted to the window, through which I could see the big cottonwood in the backyard. When he was nine he had built a tree house there during one of his many stays with us. The tree house had remained there for more than fifteen years, but it was gone now.

"Hello, Carla. I heard you were here. You're looking great."

I couldn't bring myself to return the compliment. Often when seeing a newspaper photograph of some man accused or even convicted of crime, I have been surprised at how respectable he looks, at least in the suit and tie in which his lawyer has arrayed him for his court appearance. But no amount of Brooks Brothers tailoring could have made Mahlon look like anything except what he was—a sly and unappetizing lawbreaker, with small eyes that tended to shift

96

away from one's gaze, a loose-lipped mouth, and, even though he was years past the acne age, bad skin.

"Hello, Mahlon." I hesitated, suddenly aware that anything one might say to a recently released convict—"How does it feel to be out?" or even, "Found a job yet?"—might sound offensive. And so I confined myself to a feeble, "How are you?"

"I'm doing okay." Then his voice took on that sly intonation I had always hated. "But you seem a little nervous. What's the matter? Afraid your big bad cousin is still sore at you?"

As a matter of fact I did feel a little uneasy, alone with him in this darkening house. But I tried to keep my voice calm and friendly. "No, I'm not afraid of that. My mother said just yesterday that you'd told her that was all water under the bridge."

"Sure. And anyway, you were just a kid back then."

I'd been eighteen that spring night when, home from college for the weekend, I had been awakened by a sound from the backyard. I swung out of bed and crossed to the window. I saw that it must be very late, so late that a last-quarter moon was just rising in the east. Its light was dim, but even so I could make out Mahlon's silhouetted body, thin and with slightly stooped shoulders, descending a short aluminum ladder propped against the cottonwood's trunk. Puzzled, I watched him carry the ladder to our unlocked tool shed. He emerged from the shed without the ladder and walked swiftly and quietly down the driveway.

Mahlon had not been staying in our house. Instead,

97

according to a postcard my mother had received recently, he'd been in Galveston, working on the shrimp boats. And so why had he been descending from the tree house at this predawn hour? Had he, for some mysterious reason, spent the night up there?

The next morning, a Sunday, I did not mention what I had seen to my mother. Her life had been hard enough in those days, what with widowhood (she had not yet met Chad), and her long hours behind a store counter, and her loneliness for Jennifer, living up at the mission school, and for me, away at college all week. I did not want to add to her burdens by telling her of the strange behavior of the nephew she had always doted upon. But if by any chance she left the house during the day, I would climb up and investigate that tree house.

I had no such opportunity. In the late afternoon I took the bus back to college, resolved that the next Saturday, while my mother was at work, I would investigate the tree house. But she had been gone only a few minutes that Saturday when the narcotics officers arrived. They showed me a search warrant.

Even if they had not begun their visit by questioning me about my cousin, I would have known it was some act of his that had brought them there. Before long they told me that they were looking for heroin Mahlon might have hidden in the house. I quite truthfully denied all knowledge of the heroin or of Mahlon's present whereabouts. They left me sitting in the kitchen while they ranged all over the house. I listened to their rummaging, sick with the thought

98

of what my mother would feel when she learned about this, and hoping desperately that they would just give up and leave.

They didn't, of course. Instead they came back to the kitchen for another go at me. I think they were nice men. At least, despite my fear of them, I caught an impression of decency. But they had a job, and if doing it involved bullying an eighteen-year-old college girl, then so be it.

One of them said to me, "You're holding something back, aren't you? You may not know for sure where the stuff is, or where your cousin is, but you know *something*. Don't bother to deny it. We've been lied to by experts."

The other one said, "We'll find the drugs sooner or later, with or without your help. But if you hold out on us, you can be named as an accessory. Maybe your mother can too, since she owns this place."

They didn't have to push me any harder than that. I told them about the tree house. Fifteen minutes later they drove away with the drugs.

As for Mahlon, we later learned that he had been in custody even before the narcotics agents, acting on a tip from a man who had shared his jail cell, came to search our house.

Neither my mother nor I had to testify against Mahlon. His fingerprints were all over the metal box that held the heroin, and besides, they soon had his confession. But everyone for miles around, including Martha Baron, must have known that Mahlon was my mother's nephew. True, when her son, more than a year after Mahlon's arrest, brought me home as a bride, she never mentioned my cousin to me. But her knowledge of his imprisonment must have added to her dismay over our marriage.

In another state or at another time Mahlon might have reaped a much lighter sentence for possession of what was a relatively small amount of heroin. But Arizonians had become increasingly irate over the small, low-flying planes which almost at will flew marijuana and hard drugs across the border. Mahlon was sentenced to ten years and had served nine of them.

Now I said, "I hear you've been over in El Paso."

"Yeah. Job hunting in the railroad yards there."

"Any luck?"

"No. If you're an ex-con they won't even give you a job on a track gang."

His voice had been mild, holding none of the resentment it would have been only natural for him to feel. As of old, apparently, he was being sly, covering up what he really felt.

A silence settled down. The kitchen was filling with shadows. Feeling a sudden sharp unease, I said, "I'd better set the table, so Mama won't have to do it when she and Chad get home."

Turning, I went down the hall and into the dining room. As I touched the light switch, I heard his following footsteps. I went over to the massive sideboard and opened the long drawer where plastic place mats as well as the family silverplate always had been kept. Then something made me look up at the long mirror which hung above the sideboard. Mahlon was staring at my back with a venom that

100

suggested that he would like to drive a knife between my shoulder blades.

So much for water under the bridge.

He must have become aware of my gaze, because he raised his eyes to my mirrored face and smiled. "Just came in to save you the bother of setting a place for me. Right after I got off the bus this afternoon I had a burger and a milkshake at Eddie's Diner. But tell the folks I'll be back in a few hours. Well, good to have you back, Carla."

I heard his footsteps go down the hall, out the front door.

I stood motionless. The night caller. Could Mahlon possibly have been responsible? Then again I dismissed the idea. Not that he didn't have malice aplenty. What he lacked was sufficient intelligence to engineer such a scheme.

After a moment I took out three plastic place mats and laid them on the table. I had just finished setting out the silverware when I heard the sound of Chad's car in the driveway.

12

A LITTLE AFTER seven the next night Ben Solway and I entered the dining room of the Baronsville Hotel. Stepping into that room was like going back in time. Moose heads on the dark paneled walls stared glassily down at white clothed tables, each with a caddy offering ketchup, steak sauce, and piccalilli. Interspersed with the moose heads were large framed photographs of presidents of the last sixty-odd years, from genial and handsome Harding to genial and handsome Reagan. There were only seven portraits, though. The family that ran the hotel, hard-shell Republicans all, had chosen not to display photographs of Democratic presidents.

I was feeling quite rested. My sleep in Martha Baron's guest cottage had been peaceful, so much so that in the morning, when I switched off the light I had left burning in the upstairs hall, I resolved not to leave it on the next night. With the whole ground floor locked tight, surely I need not fear physical attack. The light burning all night could only discourage a fourth early-morning phone call, and thus defeat the very purpose that had brought me out here.

I had spent the day with my mother, who could not hide her hopeful excitement at the news that I was having dinner with Ben. I'd told her how much I was in love with Mike Trenton, but it was obvious that she still envisioned me resigning from my job, bringing her grandchild out here, and settling down with Ben.

Now, seated opposite him in the hotel dining room, I reflected that there could be worse fates. Ben was so darned *nice*, with his direct blue eyes and slow, warm smile. Not a with-it person, not by Manhattan standards, but very nice indeed.

We both ordered what was listed on the menu as New York cut steak. In New York they call that sort of steak Kansas City cut. What they call it in Kansas City I don't know. Midway through the meal I asked, after a certain amount of hesitation, "No girl, Ben?"

"No one special. I wish there was." He paused and then went on. "I don't say this to make you feel bad. But after you, I couldn't find any girl in this town who really interested me."

"Then try another town. You'll find someone, sooner or later."

He smiled. "I'd better. I'm getting to be an old man. Thirty-three my next birthday."

About an hour later we left the hotel and walked out to where Ben's car was parked beside the Chevrolet I had rented from him. His car was a white Cadillac convertible, mute evidence that his garage was doing well. I'm sure my mother regarded it as evidence of how right she'd been in telling me, years ago, that Ben would turn out to be a real catch.

He said, "Like to go for a ride?"

"Very much." There are not many sources of evening entertainment in Baronsville. Two rather tacky bars. A movie theater whose current offering was a picture we both had seen. Besides, I'd always liked riding over the desert at night, with the level road racing backward beneath the headlights' beam, and the cooling air fragrant with sage. We drove for about twenty miles. The second-quarter moon had set, leaving a dark blue sky strewn with stars that appear twice as large and glittering as any I have ever seen anywhere else.

At last Ben said, "I don't suppose you'd like to stop for a while."

He was attractive, and I liked him a lot. Furthermore, I felt depressed and anxious whenever I pictured Mike's face, so grimly unsmiling the last time I had seen him. It would be comforting to exchange a few kisses with Ben. But no, it would be stupid, as well as unfair to him, to start something I was not prepared to finish.

"Best not to," I said.

After a long moment he answered, "Okay. I'll turn around at the crossroads up ahead."

When we had returned to my Chevy and I had gotten inside, Ben closed the door and then asked, "Dinner again soon?"

"I'd like that. I've enjoyed this evening very much."

He leaned down and kissed my lips lightly. "Good. I'll phone you."

I drove back to Martha Baron's place and down past the darkened main house to the cottage. Even though I had left a light burning in the living room, I felt a certain tension as I unlocked the front door. Everything seemed just as I had left it, though. To make sure, I went all over the ground floor, and then, through the silence, climbed to my room.

Three days passed. I spent hours with my mother and Chad. Out at the mission school, I shared with my sister and her charges a very creditable beef stew luncheon. Again I had dinner with Ben, this time at a new spot six miles west of Baronsville.

One afternoon, at Mrs. Baron's telephoned invitation, I went to the main house for tea and tiny sandwiches. I of course let her take the conversational lead, which meant that we talked almost entirely of Melissa. Neither of us even mentioned Melissa's father.

Twice I talked with Dodie Sims and with my daughter, who seemed so taken with the two Siamese that she gave only the most cursory attention to my questions about school, tooth brushing, and table manners.

I also called Mike twice. The second time he demanded, "When are you coming back?"

"I don't know. When I've learned something, I guess."

"And when will that be? My God, Carla. You can't

stay out there forever."

I didn't want to stay out here at all. But what was my alternative? To go back, no wiser than when I'd left, and wait for more early-morning phone calls?

When I remained miserably silent, Mike said, "Considering that neither of us have stock in the phone company, there doesn't seem much point in prolonging this conversation, does there? Good-bye, Carla."

He hung up. Wretchedly, I wondered if he had been seeing Nicole Stacey. Whether he had or not so far, if I remained away long enough he would be seeing Nicole, or, if not her, one of the few thousand other young Manhattan women who would leap at the chance to go out with him.

In the afternoon, while I helped my mother clean out the upstairs and downstairs closets, and later on watched a soap opera with her, I entertained longing thoughts about New York, and my life there with Melissa and my job and Mike.

Perhaps it was because I had been thinking for hours about New York that, in the early evening, I imagined I saw my old *bête noire* at Halstead and Sons, Jim Allerdyce.

My mother had prepared an early supper that night because the VFW, of which Chad was a member, was to hold a Ladies' Night at the Baronsville Hotel. They urged me to go with them, but I begged off, saying that I planned to wash my hair that evening. That was true, but also I refused because Mahlon was at the table that night, and I feared that if I went to the hotel with my mother and Chad he would tag along too, just because he knew I shrank from his presence.

There was still an after-sunset dazzle in the sky as I drove westward toward Martha Baron's place. Traffic on this narrow, two-way road was light. Truck traffic between the scattered small towns always dwindled toward evening, and so did the number of private cars, since most people were at table or watching TV. Thus I took more than usual notice of the few cars I did meet.

A dark red two-door, a Buick or perhaps an Oldsmobile, approached me. It seemed to slow a little as it passed, and the driver turned his face toward me, an almost emaciated face shadowed by a felt hat. Our eyes met for a second or two as we passed each other.

Jim Allerdyce, here on this back road in the Arizona desert? No, I must have been mistaken. For one thing, the man's hat brim had kept me from getting a really good look at him. For another, Allerdyce was far from being the only bony-faced man in the world.

But the incident had upset me. All the time while I was washing and blow-drying my hair, I kept reliving, more vividly than I had for days, the shock of that first early-morning phone call, and, that afternoon, the malice in Jim Allerdyce's face as he told me I looked like "death warmed over."

I lay awake for a long time that night. And when I finally did sleep I had anxiety dreams so distressing that they twice woke me up. First I dreamed that I started to edit a manuscript, bought by Halstead and Sons at my earnest recommendation, and suddenly realized that the book was written in some unknown language. After waking from that dream I went back to sleep and dreamed that I went to pick up Melissa in the late afternoon from her school. But somehow I missed my way and wandered through increasingly murky streets, searching for her school.

It was a few seconds after I had awakened from that dream that I heard the sound from somewhere below in the darkened house.

It had been a kind of crash, reverberating, and yet so muffled that probably I would not have heard it had I been asleep. As it was, I sat bolt upright in bed, ears straining. I listened for several seconds, but heard nothing except the thudding of my own heart.

I had an almost overwhelming urge to pick up the phone and call the Baronsville police. But there would have been little point in it. To judge by the sound, whoever had made it was already inside the house. And no matter which member of the four-man police force was on duty, it probably would take him at least twenty minutes to shake off his after-midnight somnolence and drive out here.

True, just the sound of my telephoning might cause the intruder to flee, without my catching even a glimpse of him. But was that what I wanted? Had I traveled almost three thousand miles, only to lose my nerve when I finally had at least a chance to learn something about my persecutor?

The luminous dial of the wristwatch I'd placed

on the bedside stand told me it was a little past two-thirty. Stomach tightened into a knot, I swung out of bed, thrust my feet into slippers, picked up my robe from a chairback and put it on. Trying to make no sound, I slid open the drawer of the bedside stand, drew out the gun and the small flashlight I'd placed beside it, and put them in the pockets of my robe. I slipped out of the bedroom and, by the faint light coming through a window at the hall's end, moved to the head of the stairs.

I hesitated, reluctant to descend into the pitch-darkness below. But I was even more afraid of turning on the upstairs hall light or even my flashlight, and not just because I might send the intruder fleeing out through whatever means of entrance he had found. He might not flee. And if he had a gun and chose to use it, the flashlight would make me an easy target. I descended slowly and carefully, hand on the railing, and thankful that in this well-built house stairs did not creak.

I had just stepped down onto the lower hall when—half relieved, half disappointed—I heard a car start up somewhere in the distance and drive away, the sound of its engine growing fainter. As nearly as I could judge, the car had been parked near the pillared entrance to the Baron property. It was most unlikely that Mrs. Baron or any of her help would have had a caller at this hour of the morning, especially one who did not drive up to the house. Almost certainly the driver of that car had been in this cottage only minutes ago.

Still, I could not be absolutely certain of that. The

car might have held lovers who had parked for a while at the roadside. And even if the driver had been the one who had broken into this house, I could not assume he had gone for good. I pictured him stopping his car, making his way back to this house on foot, peering in some ground-floor window while I made my search. . . .

It was that thought which kept me from turning on any of the house lights. By the flashlight's narrow beam, I examined the front door. Firmly locked. Still with no illumination but the flashlight, I moved from room to room. Nowhere was there a window unlocked. Nor was there an overturned piece of furniture or any other indication as to what had made that reverberating crash.

After I had shone my flashlight around the kitchen I went down the short hall beyond and looked into each of the small servants' rooms and tested the lock on the back door. When I returned to the kitchen I again shone the flashlight's beam over the long stainless-steel sink boards, the tall refrigerator, the stove and infrared wall oven, the door to the basement playroom . . .

Perhaps down there?

I opened the door as soundlessly as I could and then descended by the flashlight's beam. Down here in this windowless room there was no reason not to turn on the lights. I returned the flashlight to one pocket of my robe and, every nerve drawn tight, took that flat little gun from the other. Then I touched the switch.

By the amber glow of the wall lights I saw that

there was no one in the room but myself. Someone had been here, though. Neil's drum set as well as his guitar and its stand had been tipped over onto the thick red carpet.

So that was it. But how had he gotten in, whoever it was who had blundered into those instruments?

A creaking sound made my heart leap. It was not until then that I saw that the door in the opposite wall, the one leading from this expensively furnished playroom to the utilitarian part of the basement, stood open a few inches.

With little chills rippling down my back, I stood motionless for several seconds. No hand or face appeared in the opening, nor did the door move again. I began to relax slightly. Whoever had sent those musical instruments crashing to the floor had retreated through that doorway, neglecting in his haste to close the door properly. I was almost certain now that he had hurried straight to his car and probably was already miles away from here.

But what had made the door move?

A current of air, most likely, from an open window.

This air-conditioned playroom was windowless. What was more, I probably hadn't looked into the rest of the basement more than once or twice during the years I had lived in this house. Thus the whole belowground area had remained windowless in my memory. But now I had a sudden recollection that there *were* windows, small ones, high up.

Even though I was sure that whoever had turned over those drums was long gone, I still had to steel myself for a few seconds before I could walk over

111

and open that door wide. I stepped onto cement, then played my flashlight's beam over the rough plaster wall until I saw the light switch.

Brilliance flooded down from a big ceiling bulb, enclosed in a protective wire cage, onto the tall tube of the furnace, and the oversized hot water heater, and the storage bins around the wall holding garden furniture and numerous crates and barrels.

High on the wall opposite me were three narrow windows set in a row. The middle one was open. Beneath it stood a white wrought-iron garden chair. Just as in his hasty retreat he had not closed the door to the playroom, he also had not stopped long enough to close the window.

Climbing up on the chair, I closed and latched the window. I looked at the flanking windows. They were closed but not locked. Clutching the middle window's ledge for balance, I leaned first right and then left to lock the other two. Then I walked back to the playroom and looked down at Neil's guitar and drums.

I knew what he would have said, had he been there, about tonight's intrusion. "Some thieving Indian," he would have said, "after my liquor." I looked at the half dozen or so bottles behind the bar. Were they fewer than they had been the last time I was down here? I didn't know, for sure. But probably the intruder had blundered into those drums before he could reach the bar. Certainly that might indicate that he was drunk.

Neil himself had spent about a fourth of his waking life drunk.

Had he been here tonight? If so, what had he been in search of? Me? Or something he did not want me to find?

My gaze fastened on the door of the little set-into-the-wall cabinet beside the bar, the cabinet that held a number of keys, including the one to the room that had been Neil's and mine during our stormy married life. After that first cursory look around the room, I hadn't been in there again. Instead I had relocked the door and returned the key to the play-room cabinet.

But if Neil had returned to this house tonight to retrieve something, wasn't that object most likely among his personal possessions in that room?

I walked over to the cabinet and took the key down from its hook. No longer afraid that someone was lurking, I made my way up to the second floor, turning lights on and off as I went. I replaced the gun and flashlight in the cabinet next to my bed. Then I crossed the hall and unlocked the door of the room where, for three years, Neil and I had slept, dressed and undressed, sometimes made love, and more often quarreled fiercely.

13

I WENT THROUGH his suits and other clothing in the closet. They were in excellent order, the pockets not holding even lint, let alone anything important enough to have brought him crawling through that basement window. That, I knew, was the doing of the maids, who must have come into this room soon after we left for our "reconciliation picnic" that last day and restored his widely strewn belongings to the closet and to drawers. (The maids had obviously adored him, of course, especially Molly Birdfoot. Sometimes I had felt I was the only woman alive whom Neil could no longer charm.)

I took up his boots and his shoes and overturned and shook them. Nothing. I went through his bureau, lifting and turning each article of clothing, and searching under the paper that lined the drawers. Still nothing. That left almost no hiding place except the locked brass box, sitting on the bureau, in which he had kept cuff links and other masculine jewelry.

He'd kept the little key, as I remembered, taped to the underside of one of the two top bureau drawers. Yes, here it was.

I unlocked the box and opened the lid. As I did so the upper tray, attached by metal strips to the sides and top of the box, swung back with it. I began to remove items, some of which I remembered, from the upper tray and lay them on the bureau top. Much of this jewelry had been inherited from his father and grandfather and even great-grandfather—amethyst evening studs surrounded by tiny seed pearls, ruby cuff links, a gold nugget that once probably had dangled from his great-grandfather's massive watch chain.

The lower tray held similar items, as well as gold neck chains and a silver identification bracelet which Neil himself had bought. Soon the box was empty except for the thin blue paper that lined the box. No, not quite empty. Something lay beneath the paper.

I drew it out. A postcard. It was also a photograph of a younger Neil than the one I had married, twenty years old perhaps, his dark hair disordered, his eyes glassy, his smile lopsided. He had an arm around a girl, obviously Mexican, whose white embroidered blouse had slipped off one shoulder. Even in the black-and-white photograph one could see that her coarsely pretty face wore a thick coat of makeup. And I think that even an unsophisticated person would have guessed that she was a tart.

Behind them was a bar, somehow fake-looking, set with straw-covered wine bottles. Above the bar glittering letters, probably cardboard, dangled from a string to form the words *Bienvenido a Los Arboles.*

I turned the postcard over. No postmark. It had never been mailed. Nor had he addressed it. But he had scrawled a message:

> Dear Mother,
>   Here's Rosita, your future daughter-in-law. I'll be bringing her home any day now.
>
> > Your loving son,
> > Neil

I turned the postcard over again and looked at its face. Despite the girl's smile, there was a sad, scared look in the big dark eyes. Probably under all that goo her face had been very young, perhaps about fifteen. I felt a rush of sympathy for that poor little harlot, scarcely more than a child, and a rush of anger against Neil, who had used the girl to strike out at the mother he bitterly resented and yet depended upon.

True, he hadn't mailed the postcard. But he had kept it. Why? Because he really had been in love with that pathetic creature? Surely not. He had kept it as a kind of symbol of his rebelliousness against his mother, a rebellion he had continued to feel even as he and I lived in this house off her bounty.

Perhaps he also had kept it because of his ambivalent feelings about Mexico and Mexicans. On the one hand, he sneered at them as "wetbacks." (In fact, that was one of the politer terms he used.) On the other hand, he had been crazy about Mexican music, food, serapes, and wide, ornately trimmed sombreros. What was more, it was at his insistence that we had gotten married south of the border.

116

In the past he had sometimes reminded me of an old-time antiblack racist, leading a lynch mob one night, and the next weeping in some bar over the dear old black mammy he probably had never had.

A sudden thought held me motionless. True, if Neil was still alive, if by some chance he had escaped those swift currents and jagged boulders, he indeed might have been the one who, for some reason known only to himself, had crawled through that basement window. On the other hand, it might have been someone else, even one of those "thieving Indians" Neil was always denouncing. And in that case Neil right at this moment might be asleep in some Mexican hotel room, or drinking himself unconscious in some cantina, a self-exile these past four years from his own country and the comfortable life he had led for his first twenty-eight years.

I thought, with kindling excitement, could he be in Los Arboles right now? No, that would be too much to hope for. But if he *was* south of the border, chances were that he had at least revisited the town. Anyway, it would be a starting point for a search.

It seemed to me that Los Arboles was about sixty miles southeast of Nogales. Down in the library there were road maps which would show me the exact location. And even if the town was a little farther away, with an early enough start I could get there and back before dark. I would set the alarm for five . . .

Nerves taut, I crossed the hall to my bedroom, hoping but not expecting to get a little sleep before the alarm went off.

117

14

MOST Mexican roads, even today, are more suitable
for wooden carts and yoked oxen than for automo-
biles. But the one I was on, scarcely wider than my
rented Chevrolet, could be described as partially
paved. That is, long stretches of rutted dirt road,
sometimes set with tire-punishing rocks, alternated
with short stretches of weathered asphalt.

Most of the time I drove at less than thirty-five
miles an hour. Sometimes it was much less. Once I
was stuck behind a dilapidated truck, loaded with
crated chickens and traveling about fifteen miles an
hour. Not until we came to one of the infrequent
turnouts was I able to get past. Once, too, I found
myself behind a creaking bullock cart and its straw-
sombreroed driver. About a dozen goats, tethered
to the cart's high wooden sides like so many bleating
outriders, frustrated my attempts to pass at the turnouts. It was not until the cart and its noisy escort
turned off onto an even narrower road that I was

118

able to drive a little faster. And of course there were the times when I had to wait in a turnout until a car coming from the other direction passed me.

But despite the awfulness of the road and my nervous tension, I almost enjoyed that journey. Once for about fifty yards a roadrunner, that most ridiculous of birds, raced ahead of me with its drunkenly rolling gait, long tail switching from side to side. Once, while I was parked in a turnout, waiting for an ancient yellow bus to pass, a two-foot-long iguana lizard stared at me unwinkingly from the shade of a creosote bush, looking so fierce in its thick, shiny hide of many colors that I had to remind myself that iguanas were as harmless as baby chicks.

And always there were the magnificent clouds of Mexico. Sometimes they towered on the horizon like snowy alps. Sometimes their shadows raced over the desert earth. I would feel their coolness for a few moments before they moved on, leaving the sandy earth bathed in sunlight so brilliant that the shadows cast by everything—towering cacti, small reddish boulders, occasional adobe shacks near the roadside—looked black as ink.

It had been not quite seven o'clock when I left that opulent guest cottage. Lest Mrs. Baron wonder where I had gone at such an early hour, I stopped at the back door of the main house long enough to hand the fat Indian cook a note, addressed to Mrs. Baron and saying that I was going to "drive up to Tucson" for the day. Then I drove into town. As I had hoped, no one seemed to be up at my mother's house. I placed a similar note under the door.

119

At the far edge of town, Ben Solway was just unlocking his garage office. He saw me, but I just waved and drove on. When I reached the main highway I turned south toward Nogales, confident that I could be back across the border before nightfall.

Now, at a little past noon, I was not so sure. But according to the map, Los Arboles was only a few miles away. Soon I saw up ahead a whitewashed house, set in a grove of cottonwoods at a bend in the road. I drove around the bend and there, about a half mile ahead, was a little town I knew must be Los Arboles. Fleetingly I wondered where it had gotten its name, since Los Arboles means "the trees," and there seemed to be no trees in the area except for those cottonwoods back there. Perhaps a hundred years ago or more there had been a few desert willows here, or smoke trees, or some such.

At the town's edge I got out of the Chevy, locked it, and then, heartbeat fast, started down the main street's wooden sidewalk. I passed a general store, its windows crowded with merchandise which ranged from a purple dress of some synthetic material to a transistor radio and a green glass orange-juice squeezer. After that there was an open-fronted cantina. As far as I could tell from a quick glance into its shadowy interior, the customers at its tables were all men. But then, I had already known that in Mexico women—at least respectable women—don't go to cantinas. Next there was a combination grocery store and meat market, with a pathetic row of dead rabbits, their fur still on, dangling like executed felons from a gibbet made up of two wooden

uprights and a wooden crossbar. Next there was another open-fronted cantina and then a souvenir
store, also open-fronted, with stalls displaying striped
serapes, sombreros ranging from doll-size to three
feet across, and pottery jars and bowls.

I wasn't surprised to find a souvenir store in this
small village because already I had seen, among the
predominantly native pedestrians, a few Americans.
There had been two men of about forty, looking
quaint in their hippie-style pony tails held back by
a rubber band and their square Ben Franklin glasses.
There had been a young couple, backpackers, in
shorts and woolen socks and thick-soled shoes. And
coming toward me now was a middle-aged couple,
with determined smiles which told me they intended
to strike up a conversation.

But we never had that conversation because just
then, with a leap of my pulse, I saw another open-
fronted souvenir store across the street. This one,
according to the sign atop its wide doorway, provided not only *recuerdos*—souvenirs—but *tarjetas
postales fotografía*—photographic postcards.

I darted across the dirt street and entered the
shop. Yes, there it was, the fake bar of the postcard
with its straw wine bottles and, on the wall behind
it, giant sombrero.

A smiling fat man moved toward me. "You want
your picture taken, señorita? I put on postcard. Very
nice."

"No, thank you. But if you could give me some
information—I mean, have you been in this shop
long?"

121

He shrugged. "Twelve years, maybe fifteen."

With unsteady fingers I opened my shoulder bag and took out Neil's postcard. "Were you the one who made this picture?" I handed it to him.

He frowned at it for several moments. He turned it over and, lips moving, read the message. Then, with a chuckle, he turned it over again and looked at the picture. "Girl he was going to marry! That one good joke."

"Did you take the picture?"

Frowning again, he shrugged. "Maybe. I remember the girl, Rosita. But I don't remember— *Hola!* I do remember. An Americano, Señor Bushmill, had that *tarjeta* made long time ago, maybe first time he was in Los Arboles."

Another of Neil's little jokes. Bushmill's was his favorite brand of Irish whiskey.

The fat man added, chuckling, "Reason I no recognize him, Señor Bushmill look like *nino* in that picture. Some different now!"

My breathing, even my heartbeat, seemed to stop for a moment. So evidently my husband was still alive.

I asked, "Then he's here, in this town?"

He shook his head. "No, he just come back here sometimes."

"Then where does he live?"

"Right now? *No sabe.* Last time he was here, maybe six months ago, he tell me he was staying in Todos Santos."

"Where's that?"

"Town maybe fifty miles from here. Bigger town

than Los Arboles. You find it on map." He laughed, apparently at some recollection about Neil. "Last time he come here, he had his *novia* with him." He handed the postcard back to me.

"His sweetheart? The girl in this picture?"

"Oh, no. That Rosita, she go away with some man long time ago, to Mexico City, I think. This girl is tall, skinny girl, much older. Older than Señor Bushmill, I think."

"Do you have any idea just where in Todos Santos—"

"No, señorita." Again he laughed. "You just look in the cantinas. If he's in Todos Santos, you find him."

"Thank you very much." I put the postcard back in my shoulder bag and took out my billfold.

He said, eyeing the billfold, "You want me to make *tarjeta postale* with your picture? Pretty girl like you, you make fine *postale.*"

"No, thank you. I don't have time." I took ten dollars from my billfold and handed it to him. "But please accept this for your trouble."

"*Mil gracias,* señorita!"

While he was still beaming at the bill I left the cantina and hurried back along the dusty street to my car. From its glove compartment I took out a road map and, almost tearing it in my nervous haste, unfolded it.

Todos Santos was about fifty miles southeast of Los Arboles. To judge by the map, the road leading to it was of the same class as the one I had traveled so far.

I looked at the dashboard clock. A quarter after

two. If I turned north right now I might be able to reach Martha Baron's place by dark, or shortly thereafter. But I did not want to turn around, not with that other town—and perhaps Neil—only fifty miles away. I had an absurd but strong feeling that if I waited until some other day to go there, he might drift away from Todos Santos in the interval, and I would never find him, never be really sure whether or not I had a living husband, and whether or not it was his voice I had heard in the dark early-morning hours in that Manhattan bedroom.

Of course, if I went on, I would either have to spend the night in Todos Santos or drive back to the border in darkness over these terrible roads. But if I had to do it, so be it. I would drive very carefully. And if anyone tried to force me off the road—something that happened now and then to American tourists—I had that gun, Neil's gun, in my shoulder bag along with that postcard.

Hands cold with nervousness, I refolded the map, put it in the glove compartment and started the Chevy.

15

WHEN I reached Todos Santos I found the town *en fiesta*, although which saint they were honoring with a celebration I never knew. It was a woman saint, though. As I drove along the wide main street under strings of brightly colored electric lights, my way impeded not only by horn-tooting cars ahead of me but by laughing, shouting pedestrians who darted from sidewalk to sidewalk, I saw the saint being carried on a weaving course through the traffic. Clad in a yellow robe, and with dark hair framing her plaster face, she was seated in a chair atop a platform carried by four sturdy-looking young men.

Except for that saintly image, the town seemed much like a miniature Las Vegas, minus the neons and the tall buildings. From the open-fronted cantinas sambas and salsas and rhumbas and occasional plaintive ballads poured out to mingle with the blaring horns and the shouts and the laughter. As the Chevy crept along, I kept looking from side to side, taut with the expectation of seeing Neil somewhere in the street crowd.

I did not. At the far end of the street I managed to angle my car over to the curb. I got out and tried the doors to make sure they were locked. Then I started down the sidewalk.

Although I had expected to be here before sunset, it was now almost eight and fully dark. The road, even worse than the one between the border and Los Arboles, had been responsible. Twice I had come to rickety bridges across dry arroyos. I had not needed the wooden signs, *Despacio! Peligroso!*—Slow! Dangerous!—to make me reduce speed. At about five miles an hour I crept across.

But if I'd had bad luck where the road was concerned, I experienced an extraordinary stroke of good luck now. If I just looked in the cantinas, the fat man had told me, I would find Señor Bushmill. And I did find him, in the first cantina I came to.

Wearing white trousers and an open-throated Mexican-style white shirt, and holding a glass in his hand, he sat alone at a table near one side of the shedlike structure. On the table stood a small oil lamp with a red glass shade, the same sort of lamp I had seen in souvenir shop windows in Los Arboles. It sent a glow over his face and the lock of dark hair falling over his forehead. As I moved forward, still not quite able to believe that I had actually found him, I thought, how very handsome he still is.

Heart pounding, dimly aware that men at the other scattered tables were staring at the bold *norteamericana,* I stopped beside Neil. He raised his

126

head. For several seconds he regarded me with an expression of stunned incredulity.

Now that I was close, I saw that his appearance had changed more than I had thought at first. His face was puffier. And there were scars. One on his upper lip, another at the corner of his left eye, giving the lid a slightly Oriental slant. No doubt by daylight other scars would be visible. Nevertheless, he was still a handsome man.

And still very self-possessed. No longer wearing that stunned look, he got to his feet. "Hello, Carla."

Unable to speak, I nodded.

"Have a seat."

I sat down in the chair opposite his own. He too sat down and then said, "So you hired yourself some detectives. How long have they been looking for me?"

I found my voice. "No detectives." A sudden rage made my voice shake. "Anyway, I should think that I'm the one with the right to ask questions."

"The right? Oh, I don't know what rights you've got, a wife who doesn't lift a finger to keep her husband from drowning."

So after he slid into that torrent, he had not been too drunk to remember that I just stood there. Perhaps the shock of the icy water and the perception of his danger had sobered him almost instantly.

"But you didn't drown."

For the first time since I came in, he smiled. "No, I didn't, did I? You want a drink?"

I did not, but I feared that if I refused he would turn sullen and silent, and so I nodded and said,

"Whatever you're having will be okay."

He looked past my shoulder toward the bar, pointed to his glass, and held up two fingers. Then he asked, "Like some music?"

I gripped my hands together in my lap. "What sort of music?"

"Didn't you notice the jukebox when you came in? It's a genuine 1940s antique."

He got up and walked a few feet to where the jukebox stood in the cantina's rear corner. He fed a coin into the gaudily lighted machine and then waited until "La Cucaracha" blared forth to mingle with the sound of automobile horns and strolling bands out in the street.

He started back to the table just as the bartender, a thin, fortyish man with a pockmarked face, set down two full glasses and removed Neil's empty one. Evidently Neil had decided to stop toying with me because he said, when the bartender had withdrawn, "No, light of my life, I didn't drown. I don't know how come. After I went over the falls I got knocked around plenty among the sharp rocks. I was too numb to feel it much, but I knew I was getting pretty cut up. Still, I managed to stay alive through the rapids and into a quiet stretch."

He took a long swallow of his drink, set the glass down. "The current was still too swift for me to swim across it toward shore," he said, "but I angled that way gradually, letting my feet down every once in a while. And finally, God knows how much later or how far downstream, I was able to wade ashore. I staggered across a strip of sand and into the pines

128

and collapsed there."

Again he lifted his glass and drank. I took a sip of my own drink. It was some kind of whiskey mixed with soda.

"After a while I checked to see what shape I was in. I knew I had lots of cuts but evidently the cold water had sealed the minor ones. The only one still bleeding much was on my right leg. I tore off part of my shirttail and made a tourniquet. After that, Carla, my dear little Carla, I just lay there for a while and thought of how much I hated you, and my mother, and my marriage, and my whole damned life."

I thought of him lying there, cut and battered, delivered from the river's grasp, but still in the grip of his own demons. I wanted to cry out, "Did you hate your daughter, too?" but I knew I had better not, lest he stop talking.

He said, "And then it dawned on me. I didn't have to go on with my life. I was officially dead now. Sure, when they dragged the river they wouldn't find my body. But in the case of several people who had just disappeared in that stretch of water, the verdict had been 'presumed drowned.' What was more, I had thirty thousand in a Tucson bank, enough to start a nice new life for myself."

I said, astounded, "You had money in a Tucson bank?" I always had thought that the only savings Neil and I had were in a joint account in the Baronsville bank. It was the money in that account, about three thousand dollars, which had taken Melissa and me to New York and bought us food and shelter

129

until I found a job.

He grinned at me. "Sweetie, I had what every married man ought to have, money the little woman doesn't know about."

I warned myself not to react to his needling. I asked, in a mild tone, "But how? Where did you get the money?" Certainly the salary his mother paid him for being her business manager's assistant was generous, especially considering how little work he did, but I was sure it had not enabled him to save that much money.

"From the mater, my deah, deah mater. I told her several times that I was in hock to the Las Vegas bookies. Each time, after lecturing me for half an hour, she came through, lest her little boy be dumped in a roadside ditch with bullet holes in him."

I said, in that same mild voice, "But you hadn't lost to the bookies."

"No, I've always been lucky at picking pro-football winners. The few times I laid money down in Vegas I won. But nearly all of that thirty thousand was money I'd gotten from mommie dearest. I lay there under the pines, thinking of what I could do with it."

Dimly I was aware of our surroundings. Some man bellowing with laughter as he leaned across the bar toward the bartender. Two men arguing in rapid Spanish—something about a lottery ticket—at a nearby table. Two more men and a heavily painted girl wandering in off the sidewalk. But nearly all of my attention was centered on Neil's account of that afternoon more than four years in the past.

He said, "I figured that if I walked a few miles paralleling the river, I'd come to the bridge."

I knew the one he meant. The road that crossed it was not the narrow two-lane one that ran through Baronsville but a highway, four lanes wide and with a cement divider, that ran north to Tucson.

"Even though my clothes were almost dry and the cuts on my face had stopped bleeding, I knew I must look pretty weird. Just the same, I figured I'd get a ride if the right kind of driver came along."

"And what kind would that be?"

"A woman, sweetie pie. A smart guy can always find some woman to help him out. He won't even have to look very hard."

He had reached the bridge and crossed it, he told me, and then kept on, praying that no one from Baronsville would come along and recognize him. A truck stopped to pick him up, but he waved it on.

"Then this powder-blue Buick, brand-new, drove slowly past me and then pulled up at the side of the road a few yards ahead. The driver was a brunette, around forty and not bad looking. When she swung back the door I said, 'Oh, no, lady! I've been in an accident, sort of, and I'm all messed up. I'll wait for a truck. I don't want to get your nice new car dirty.'

"She said, 'Don't be silly,' and reached into the back seat for her raincoat and spread it on the seat beside her and told me to get in.

"She asked me how I'd gotten hurt. I told her two wetbacks had jumped me when I parked my

131

car at a rest stop. They'd carved me up a little and then driven off in my car. She said, 'You poor boy!' and asked if they'd taken my wallet too. I said no, I'd had time to drop it outside the car when I saw them coming at me. When they didn't find a wallet on me they settled for taking my car.

"She was terribly indignant, of course. She said we'd stop at the first police barracks and report it. I asked her not to stop. I didn't want to get my name in the papers, I said. Finally I told her that I'd been on the lam from this girl, a girl I could never love in a million years, but who'd tricked me into agreeing to marry her. All I wanted, I said, was to get to Tucson, check into a hospital to get my cuts treated, draw out some money I had in a bank there, and keep moving.

"She ate that up, of course. Then Dorothy—Dorothy Barret, her name was—told me about herself. Since her divorce from a Florida real estate subdivider she'd just been wandering around, living off what I later learned was pretty nice alimony."

I longed to say, "That was certainly your lucky day, wasn't it?" but I checked the impulse.

"Before Dorothy and I got to Tucson I knew we were going to team up. I had some stitches taken in an emergency hospital while she bought some new clothes for me. I drew my money out of the bank. Then we headed south."

"To Mexico?"

"Sure. I told her I'd always liked Mexico, and by that time she wouldn't have cared where we went, as long as it was together. We went to Acapulco

132

first and then over to Mazatlán. There we had a really bad row and split up. I didn't mind. She'd begun to act like a wife, lecturing me about my drinking. And I didn't need her. I let her think I'd had only a few hundred bucks in that Tucson bank. She'd paid all our bills, so I still had nearly all of the thirty thousand. I started drifting around on my own. I've been here in Todos Santos for about eight months now."

I said, "There can't be much of the thirty thousand left, not after four years. Even in Mexico living isn't that cheap."

"Oh, I've been able to make a little money. Right now I'm managing this girl who sings at the Casa Encantada. That's a kind of resort about five miles from here. You know how I've always been crazy about Mexican music."

He looked at my glass, which was still nearly full, and then held up one finger to the bartender. When the man had placed a full glass before him and removed the empty one, Neil said, "All right, Carla. Your turn. How did you even know I was alive?"

16

I STUDIED the handsome face. Despite the fact that he had been drinking steadily since I sat down at the table, and for heaven only knew how long before that, he was far from drunk. I said evenly, "I knew you were alive because you began calling me up in New York at three and four o'clock in the morning."

He said, after a silence of several moments, "When did *you* go on the sauce?"

"Come off it, Neil."

"*You* come off it. I didn't even know you were in New York. For all I knew, you'd stayed right there in Baronsville and married that grease monkey who was so crazy about you. What was his name? Ben Holloway?"

"Solway." I thought of adding, "And he owns a prosperous garage and a Cadillac." I also thought of asking, "And it wouldn't have bothered you in the least, learning that I had entered a bigamous

134

marriage?" But no, I mustn't let him get me side-tracked.

"Neil, you did call me, three times. I wasn't drunk any of those times, or hallucinating, or anything like that. After the second call I notified the police and the telephone company. Your third call was monitored, but you hung up before it could be traced."

He drained his glass and signaled the bartender. "Just what did I say during those phone calls?"

"You begged me to come back to you. You promised me you'd stop drinking. And the last time you called you suggested we meet up by the river. You mentioned that night before we were married, that night when there was a full moon . . ."

His eyes had become a little glassy now. Still, I saw something flicker in them. Had a memory actually stirred a response in him? A memory of a night seven years in the past when we had first made love, there on a blanket spread on pine needles, and with an enormous white moon shining down through the branches. A night before all the quarrels began, and we still loved each other. Or at least I had loved him, with all the bedazzled ardor of first love.

He took a long swallow of his drink. When he next spoke his voice was matter-of-fact. "Carla, now that you've found me, how can you still believe that I called you up and begged you to come back to me? I'll level with you. I don't believe I've even thought of you more than once or twice in the past year."

I had long since ceased to love him, and yet that stung, somehow. "And Melissa? Have you thought of her?"

His gaze seemed to flinch slightly. Again I had touched a nerve. But his reply was indirect. "I was never cut out to be a father." After a moment he added, "Is she okay?"

"She's fine. She's back in New York with a friend of mine."

There was a brief silence. Then: "What on earth gave you the idea it was me calling you?"

"It was your voice, Neil."

"You mean, it was somebody imitating me." The mocking note was back in his voice. "Somebody who really doesn't like you, honeybun. Now come on, tell me how you tracked me down."

After a moment I said, "In the first place, for about a week now I've been staying in the guest cottage."

He looked at me incredulously. "You mean, where you and I lived?"

"Yes. After I flew out to Arizona to—to try to find out the truth about those phone calls, your mother suggested that I stay in the cottage."

"I'll be damned." I expected him to ask how his mother was, or at least to ask some sort of question about her, but he did not. "Okay. Go on."

"Last night, about three in the morning, someone crawled in through a basement window and then went into the playroom. I heard a noise and went down to investigate, but by that time the person was gone." I paused. "I thought it was probably you."

He laughed. "I don't remember for sure where I was at three o'clock last night. But I do know that until past midnight I was right here in this chair. So it isn't likely that it was me who broke in, is it?"

When I didn't answer he said, "Well, go on."

I told him about going upstairs to make another search of the bedroom we'd shared, and about finding the postcard in his jewelry box. "On the front of it was a photograph of you and some girl, standing at a fake-looking bar with a sign, *Bienvenido a Los Arboles,* hanging above it. And on the back of it there was a—a message to your mother."

He said slowly, "My God! Was that postcard still there? I had it made at least a dozen years ago, long before you and I got together. I didn't get up nerve enough to mail it to her, but I kept it to remind me that I'd *almost* had the nerve—" He broke off and then said, "So you must have driven down to Los Arboles."

"Yes. I found the place where the postcard was made. The man there remembers you, not only from twelve years ago, but from a few months ago."

Neil nodded. "I was there last November, with Manuela. She's this—client of mine, this girl singer I mentioned."

"The man in Los Arboles even remembered the name of the girl you'd posed with for that card."

"That's more than I do."

"It was Rosita. But he spoke of you as Señor Bushmill."

Neil grinned. "Bernard Bushmill. I took that name after it occurred to me that my mother or you or somebody might get the notion I was still alive and hire detectives to find out. I mean, I've always worried that someone who knew me might turn up down here and recognize me, in spite of what the river

137

did to my face. I figured changing my name would make things just a little harder for anyone trying to track me down."

He paused again and then said, "So the fat guy must have told you I was in Todos Santos."

"He said that was where you were staying when he last saw you. So I came here."

Neither of us spoke for a while. Out in the street a string of firecrackers went off, their sharp reports cutting through the din of automobile horns and mariachi music.

He said, "So you found me. Okay. What now?"

"Neil, are you absolutely certain you didn't make those phone calls?"

"Listen. Wheel in your stack of Bibles. I'll swear on them."

Was he telling the truth? With Neil you could never be sure. But I had the feeling he had told the truth. And if so, I thought, feeling chilled despite the night's warmth, then there was someone else out there, someone who, in Neil's phrase, really didn't like me.

I said, "I know I've aroused hostility in a few people. Who hasn't? But I don't think I've given anyone reason to hate me *that* much, except possibly my cousin Mahlon."

"The jailbird? But he's still locked up, isn't he?"

"No. He's been out on parole for several months now. But no matter how big a grudge he has against me, I don't think that he's bright enough to engineer something like those phone calls."

Neil shrugged. "Well, if you don't know who may

138

be doing it, I sure as hell don't."

Someone had put another coin in the jukebox. Again "La Cucaracha" burst forth, mingling with the noise from outside. Neil and I said nothing for a while. Then he asked, "Anything else on your mind?"

"Yes. There's a man I want to marry."

"Ben What's-his-name?"

"No, not Ben. A man in New York. But I can't marry him when I have a living husband. There are laws about that."

Neil smiled. "Since I don't imagine you expect me to kill myself, you must be talking about a divorce. Sure, happy to oblige. Have a lawyer send me any sort of papers that are necessary. My present finances don't run to alimony, though."

"I don't need or want alimony. Just the divorce."

Not answering, he directed his gaze past me. I turned and looked. A tall, thin woman in a yellow blouse and a tight black skirt of some shiny material was walking toward us.

Neil said, not bothering to rise, "*Hóla,* Manuela." He added, in Spanish so rapid that I could scarcely follow it, "Pull up a chair. This is Carla, a friend of mine from the North."

The woman sat. Neil turned to me. "This is Manuela. She's never learned much English. We can talk about anything we like."

I smiled and nodded at the woman. She was about thirty-five, with dark straight hair pulled back into a chignon and dressed with a tortoise comb. In her thin, high cheekboned face her mouth was surprisingly full-lipped. That heavily rouged mouth, and the tight, low-cut yellow blouse, and a certain weight of experience in her dark eyes made me think that Manuela made money by means other than singing.

She returned neither my nod nor my smile, but just stared at me with eyes which were both hostile and frightened. I thought, with a twist of sympathy, how very much she must love her handsome *norteamericano*.

Apparently he noticed her expression, because again he spoke in Spanish so rapid that I caught only a phrase or two—"just a friend," and "here only for a few hours." Manuela seemed to relax a little, although she still did not smile.

Neil looked at me. "Where were we?"

"We were talking about divorce."

"That's right. I'll cooperate in every way. But in return, you've got to promise me something."

"What?"

"Promise not to tell my mother where I am, or even that I'm alive."

I felt a little sick. How awful to return to Martha Baron's place without telling her that her son was alive! And yet would it be a kindness for anyone to let her know that her son—her handsome and so-beloved son—was now just an alcohol-soaked pimp with a scarred face, spending his days and nights in a south-of-the-border cantina? Even more devastating would be the knowledge of how much he hated her, so much that he had been willing to let her believe that he had died by drowning.

There was one more reason, a selfish one, for my

140

not telling her the truth. If she learned he was alive she would try to get in touch with him immediately. And then he would disappear again, perhaps so effectively that I would never find him, and would not be able to get my divorce until enough years had passed for him to be declared legally dead.

I said miserably, "That's a terrible thing to ask of me."

"Why so? She's thought of me as dead for the past four years. She must have gotten used to the idea by now."

There was some merit in his argument. I was sure she still grieved for Neil. But by this time she must have learned to live with her grief.

I said, "But don't you think that someday you may want to go to her?"

He smiled. "Okay. If it makes you feel better to think that I might, then go ahead. It could even be that I may run back to the maternal embrace, if the going gets really rough."

After a moment I asked, "How can a lawyer get in touch with you?"

"Right here. The owner here, a guy named Guerrero, keeps all my mail and messages for me whether I'm in Todos Santos or not."

For a few moments he searched the pockets of his white cotton shirt and trousers. Then he turned and from the wall behind him took down a rectangle of flimsy pink paper which bore an advertisement for lottery tickets. "Got a pen?"

I handed him a ballpoint pen from my shoulder bag.

141

He turned the pink paper over and wrote for perhaps a couple of minutes. Then he handed the paper to me. He had written his address—Bernard Bushmill, care of Eduardo Guerrero, Cafe Parajo, Todos Santos, Sonora, Mexico—and then under that a statement: "I, Neil Baron, a.k.a. Bernard Bushmill, do hereby state that I will not oppose any divorce proceedings brought against me by my wife, Carla Jackson Baron." Underneath was his signature and the date.

He said, "I'm giving you this just in case. By the time your lawyer gets in touch with me, I may be having a bad case of the d.t.'s, or be otherwise *non compos mentis.*"

He smiled as he said it, but fleetingly I'd seen utter wretchedness in his eyes. For the first time in years I felt a twinge of pity for him.

I put the sheet of pink paper in my shoulder bag and then sat there, looking down at the half inch or so of brownish liquid in my glass. I didn't know what Neil was thinking, but all sorts of memories of him were going through my mind. How scared and angry he had looked the night I was pregnant, and yet how, when Melissa was born, he'd had red roses delivered to the hospital every day, so many roses that the nurses, hunting for suitable bowls and vases, had become annoyed. I thought of how, the night we celebrated Melissa's first birthday he hadn't drunk at all. And yet, only days later, infuriated by her crying, he had seized her tiny shoulders and shaken her. He might have hurt her badly if I hadn't launched myself at him and raked fingernails down his face.

I raised my eyes from my drink and looked at him. Not much point in wondering now what he thought. Probably he had no coherent ones at all. He looked as if he had passed abruptly, as he had so often in the old days, from near sobriety to the brink of unconsciousness.

I said, "Neil! Where can I stay tonight?"

"Stay?"

"Yes! Here in Todos Santos. There must be a hotel."

He laughed. "You wanna stay in a hotel? Here, in fiesta time, a girl all by herself?"

"Neil! Please! Why not?"

"I'll tell you why not. Every man in town is stoned, that's why not. Even the *policía*. You wanna whole parade of men trying to get into your room all night?"

I cried, "Then what can I do?"

"Motel, just this side of Los Arboles."

"Yes, I remember passing it."

"Be pretty safe for you. *Turistas* stay there."

Only pretty safe. And anyway, if I had to go that far, I might as well go the rest of the way to Baronsville. True, the roads were terrible, but at least I had been over them once and so knew where the worst spots were. And although I should have felt exhausted, I did not. Evidently I had moved beyond tiredness to what is called a second wind.

As for the possibility that someone between here

143

and the border might try to force me off the road, I still had that gun.

I looked at Manuela. *"Buenas noches, señorita."*

She didn't smile, but some of the hostile fear left her eyes. The *gringa* did not plan to take her man from her. Instead she would go away.

I stood up. "Neil, I'm leaving now."

Head slumped on his chest, he didn't answer.

I looked for a moment more at the man who had fathered my little girl. Then I turned and walked out.

17

THE MOON was down by the time I turned in between the stone gateposts at the entrance to Martha
Baron's drive.

It had been a three-quarter moon. Its light, mingled with that of my headlamps, had guided me back
across those rickety bridges, past the darkened motel
outside Los Arboles, and through the sleeping little
town itself. Wide doors of corrugated metal now hid
the cantinas, and no one moved along the sidewalks.
The only sound was the barking of a dog somewhere
along one of the straggling side streets.

Now and then as I continued north I saw, nerves
tightening, the headlights of an approaching car. But
each time it passed me harmlessly. Soon I again
would get the feeling that I was the only human
being who moved, under that declining moon, across
a dreamlike landscape dotted with creosote bushes
and grotesque cacti and the shadows they cast.

The guards on the United States side of the border

145

eyed me suspiciously, probably because the hour was well past midnight and I was a young woman alone. After they had inspected my driver's license they asked me to get out of the car. For about five minutes they looked through the trunk and under the seats and in the glove compartment. Finally one of them, a middle-aged man, asked me to hand him my shoulder bag. He found the little gun, of course.

"You got a permit for this?"

I said yes, nerves tight with the anxiety that he might ask to see it. "But when I left early this morning I forgot to bring it with me."

He didn't question that. "I guess it's best you carry a gun, if you're going to drive in Mexico at night all by yourself."

After that preamble, I expected him to ask why I had done such a damned fool thing. If he did, I decided, I would tell him at least part of the truth. I would say, "I was looking for my husband," and hope that an official distaste for becoming involved in domestic troubles would keep him from asking more. But as it turned out I didn't have to tell him anything. He just said, "Okay" and waved me on.

Perhaps it was because I now felt that I was almost home. Whatever the reason, within a minute or two after I drove away from the immigration officials, the alertness which had sustained me all the way from Todos Santos deserted me, and I felt an overwhelming desire to pull over to the roadside and go to sleep. Instead I continued through Baronsville, as silent in the predawn darkness as that Mexican village had been, and then drove the final four miles to Martha Baron's estate.

I piloted the Chevy past the darkened main house toward the guest cottage and then took a sharp right turn into the driveway that led to the garage.

A car stood there. With my reaction time slowed by fatigue, I almost ran into it.

I braked. My headlights bathed the rear end of the car, a dark green sedan. I fumbled, panic-stricken, with the clasp of my shoulder bag. Then the car's door opened, and Mike Trenton emerged into the glare of my headlights.

Inexplicably, for a few moments longer my heart thudded with fear. Then I opened the Chevy's door with one hand, switched off the lights with the other, and ran to him. His arms closed around me.

"Where in hell have you been?"

"Mexico. Mike, I found him."

His arms tightened their grasp. After a moment he said, "Who? Your husband?"

"Yes. Why are you here, Mike?"

"Because I got too worried about you to stay back in New York. It got so I couldn't sleep nights. Let's go into the house. You're shivering."

I realized I was, but whether the cause was the predawn chill or my overstrained nerves I didn't know. We went around to the front of the house. When I had unlocked the door and turned on the light in that spacious hall, Mike looked around him and gave a low whistle, but otherwise made no comment.

In the library we sat down on the leather couch. Mike said, "God, you look awful. You look as if you

147

hadn't slept for weeks."

I said, "I feel that way too," although as a matter of fact his presence seemed to have dispelled some of my fatigue. Studying him, I saw that he too showed signs of strain. His gray eyes were slightly reddened, and tired lines had carved themselves into his face.

I asked, "How long have you been waiting here?"

"Hours. I got to the Tucson airport early this evening—last evening, I mean—and rented a car there. In Baronsville a man at the garage told me how to get to Martha Baron's place."

I wondered fleetingly if it was Ben Solway who had given him directions, and if so, whether he had guessed that it was me rather than Mrs. Baron whom the stranger wanted to see.

"It was about nine when I got out here. A maid at the main house left me standing on the doorstep while she went to see her boss. She came back with the word that Mrs. Baron had gone to bed and couldn't see me. What's more, all she knew was that 'young Mrs. Baron' had left a note that morning saying that she would be away all day. I waited for a couple of hours beside the road, but then some county cops came by and told me to drive on. Maybe they were afraid I was planning a spot of burglary. Anyway, I drove down the road a few miles and then turned back and parked in your driveway."

After a moment he added, "Until I talked to that Indian maid, I had no idea you were staying in a house all by yourself. I thought you were with Neil's mother."

"I was afraid you'd worry if you knew I was alone

148

here in the guest cottage."

"Damn right I would have." He paused, and then said, "Okay. Now fill me in."

I did. I told him about the unknown intruder, and about my discovery of that postcard photograph Neil had posed for in Los Arboles. I told of finding him in that cantina in Todos Santos, scarred of face but indisputably alive.

"Had someone hauled him out of the river?"

"No, he got himself out. And then he hitched a ride with some woman, and eventually they went to Mexico."

"And he's been down there ever since?"

"Yes, just floating around. Right now he's got this girl, or rather, woman— But that isn't important. The important thing is that he's promised not to oppose a divorce."

I brought out that piece of flimsy pink paper and handed it to him. "Here's what he wrote."

Mike studied the paper for several moments. Perhaps it was just his own fatigue, but it seemed to me that his face had an odd, impassive look.

Finally, he handed it back to me. "That'll be great, if he lives up to his promise."

"I think he will. Why shouldn't he?"

"Hell, how can you know what goes through the head of a guy like that, a guy who lets you think for four years that you're a widow, and then starts calling you up in the middle of the night and begging you to come back to him—"

"He didn't make those calls."

"What?"

149

"He didn't make those calls. He says he didn't, and I believe him."

Those slightly bloodshot eyes regarded me for a long moment. Then: "All right. We can talk about that at some future time. Right now the thing for us to do is to get back to New York, see a divorce lawyer—"

"Mike, didn't you hear me? It wasn't Neil who made those phone calls. And I'm going to stay right here until I find out who it was."

"Carla, for God's sake! I still think it was Neil Baron who made those calls, but even if it was someone else, what makes you so sure he's out here? Those calls could just have easily originated in New York."

"I think he's here," I said stubbornly. "I think he's somewhere very close. It's a feeling I have."

Anger was kindling in those reddened eyes. "You're not going to give me that bilge about woman's intuition, are you?"

"Yes, I am. Maybe not woman's intuition, but intuition all the same."

"Nonsense!"

I forced my tired brain to produce an argument. "I read somewhere that what we call intuition is based on facts. The thing is, the conscious mind isn't yet aware of those facts, just the subconscious mind."

"Carla, get some sleep. Sleep until midafternoon. We'll catch the evening plane back to New York."

"Mike, I told you. There's somebody who hates me, hates me enough to try to make my life a hell. I have to find out who it is."

"Why do you have to find out? Whoever made

150

those calls probably won't do it again. And anyway, you'll have me to protect you. Isn't that enough?"

I said wretchedly, "Mike, it's just as I told you in New York. If I had only myself to think of, maybe I would do as you ask. But there's Melissa. What if he takes it into his head to strike at me through her? No matter where we went, that fear would go with me. Even years from now, if she was late coming home from school, say . . ."

My voice trailed off. He said harshly, "What it boils down to is that you don't trust me to protect you and Melissa, even though when we married she'd be my daughter too."

"Mike—"

"I don't suppose you even want me to stay out here."

I shook my head. "Please, please try to understand. With you out here, there'd be less chance that—that whoever's doing these things will come out in the open and let me know who he is."

"So you're going to stay out here alone in this house, like some poor goat tied up as bait for a tiger."

"Mike, I can't live in fear for the rest of my life. I have to do this for my sake, and for Melissa's."

He stood up. "I hoped that this time you'd listen to me. But I can see you won't."

I went with him out into the hall. At the door he said, "If you come to your senses, let me know."

Without kissing me good-bye or even touching me, he turned and went out. Even though he closed the door quietly, to me the sound was a chillingly definite one. I heard his car start up and then circle onto

151

the side lawn to get past the Chevy.

Beneath my weariness I felt a bleak desolation. He had flown three thousand miles and then waited out in the darkness for me hour after hour, only to be rebuffed. How long would he go on waiting for me to come to my senses, as he called it? Certainly not forever.

Then I was aware of nothing but my mind and body's overwhelming need for sleep. I climbed the stairs and fell, fully clothed, onto my bed.

18

THE TELEPHONE's ringing brought me up from the depths of sleep. For a moment I lay with eyes still closed. I had a numb, confused sense that I was back in Manhattan, in the dark early-morning hours, and that when I lifted the phone I would hear . . .

I opened my eyes to find brilliant Arizona sunshine flooding through the windows. Still only half awake, I reached out for the phone.

It was my mother calling. "Carla, what's been happening? I telephoned you at eight last night and got no answer—"

"I hadn't gotten back yet."

"So I figured. I thought you'd probably stayed in Tucson to have supper with Althea." Althea Carson, my best friend in college, for the last half dozen years had lived with her husband in Tucson. "So I decided to wait until you came over here this morning. But here it is, past nine o'clock. I mean, are you all right?"

153

Groggily I told her that I was.

"Did you and Althea have a good time?"

"Mother, please! I'll tell you later today. Right now I'm dead for sleep."

"All right, honey. Come over as soon as you feel up to it." We both hung up.

Now that I was awake, I decided I had better undress. I stripped off my clothes, crawled under the light blanket, and went back to sleep.

When I next awoke, the slant of the light told me it must be midafternoon. I looked at the clock on the dressing table. Past three. After calling my mother to say that I would be there in an hour, I showered and dressed. By that time it was almost four. Almost six in New York. Melissa would be home from school.

At the thought of my daughter I felt a wave of anxiety. I knew that its cause probably was nothing more than the strain I had been under for the past forty-eight hours. Nevertheless, I felt an overwhelming need to hear her voice.

Dodie answered the phone. Perhaps she heard the anxiety in my tone, because after a routine exchange of how-are-you's she handed the phone to my daughter.

Flotsam, it seemed, was going to have to have "a n'operation." Kidney stones. I kept interrupting her account of Flotsam's malaise with inquiries about her own health and her schoolwork. Finally she said, "Mama, you don't even listen. I don't think you really care about Flotsam's kidneys." After that I made no more interruptions.

When my daughter and I rang off I again looked at the clock. Ordinarily Mike would be in his apartment by now. But perhaps whatever plane he'd caught in Tucson today hadn't reached New York yet. Anyway, I thought wretchedly, what would be the point in another wrangle with him, this time over long distance?

As my mother apologetically pointed out, the meal she served that night wasn't "much of a supper." Canned spaghetti and meatballs, frozen green beans, and canned peaches for dessert. Supper was skimpy, she explained, because she'd been busy all day cooking for Chad's birthday celebration, to be held the next night.

I didn't mind the canned spaghetti. I was just grateful that my cousin Mahlon wasn't there. He had gotten a job as night man, my mother told me, at a gas station in Harlsburg, a much larger town about fifteen miles away. "But tomorrow is his night off," my mother said, "so he'll be here for Chad's party."

My mother and Chad asked me, of course, about "my day with Althea" in Tucson. By then I'd had time to make up a story. I described a shopping trip, and a fairly late dinner, and then, on the way back, a flat tire which had delayed me for some time. Both of them seemed to accept my story.

The next day I helped my mother for several hours with preparations for the party. We iced the cake and then, in honor of Chad's days in Gower Gulch, placed atop it the tiny plastic figure of a cowboy she had bought at the variety store. We extended blue and yellow paper streamers from the old-fashioned droplight above the dining room table to the corners of the room. In the living room, above the fake fireplace that held the gas heater, we put up a banner which some of Jennifer's younger pupils had made. It said, in red crayoned letters, "Happy Birthday, Chad."

While I helped my mother with those innocently joyous preparations, I thought of Neil in that Mexican cantina, and of my perhaps final quarrel with Mike, and of the shadowy figure, whoever he was, who for months had haunted my life. Thank heaven, I thought, looking at my mother's absorbed face, that she knew nothing of all that. I hoped fervently that she would never know, that she could go on enjoying a long-delayed happiness with Chad.

Early in the afternoon I went home to wash my hair and to press a dark blue silk dress, the only one I'd brought with me which was suitable for parties. As I moved from that upstairs bedroom to the ironing board in the kitchen and back, I kept thinking of Mike. I could almost see him, bent over a typewriter in his office at *Nation's Week*. . . .

Finally I gave in and called his number. Mr. Trenton was not in his office today, a feminine voice told me. No, she didn't know where he was. I hung up and dialed his apartment. No answer.

Where was he? Well, it didn't matter. Wherever he was, he must be all right. Mike could take care of himself. And if I had managed to reach him, we would have started wrangling again.

156

Unless—chilling thought—he had decided that there was no longer any point in arguing with me.

Chad's birthday party was a nice one. Even I, despite my worries, and despite my cousin's unattractive presence, found myself enjoying it. Four of the neighbors were there, and Jennifer, and Ben Solway. (Not consulting me, my mother had invited him, with an intent that was obvious to me if not to Ben.) At the dining room table, extended to its fullest length, my mother and I served a veritable feast of roast beef and stuffed potatoes and brussels sprouts and pickled beets, with the decorated cake plus strawberry ice cream for dessert.

Afterward, in the living room, those who chose to sipped hard cider Chad himself had made, and a neighbor who had brought his harmonica with him played Sousa marches and even "The Flight of the Bumblebee." Around nine Chad left the room to prepare for his Carmen Miranda number.

When he returned he wore some old white wedgies of mine which dated from my college days, his long feet extending back over the crushed-down counters. To keep the shoes from falling off, he had tied cord under the soles and over his insteps. He had rolled up his trouser legs to reveal hairy shins and draped a red-and-white checked tablecloth around him, sarong fashion. On his grizzled head he'd placed the basket of wax fruit my mother had kept on the dining room sideboard for as long as I could remember. One hand holding the fruit basket in place, fingers of his other hand snapping, hips

157

switching from side to side, he uttered a rhythmic "Shee-shee-sha-*boom*-cha! Shee-shee-sha-*boom*-cha!"

Corny? Nothing could have been cornier. But it was surefire funny, too. I noticed that my sister, like me, was wiping tears of laughter from her eyes. And my mother, who must have seen her husband do Carmen Miranda at least a dozen times, was laughing as heartily as if the experience were entirely new to her.

Then, with the harmonica player picking up the melody, Chad began to sing: "Souse of see bor-dair down May-he-co way."

My laughter abruptly died. That had been one of Neil's favorite songs. Accompanying himself on his guitar, he had recorded "Down Mexico Way" in the basement playroom, along with "La Paloma," "La Golondrina," and, of course, "La Cucaracha." I had stayed down there with him for a little while that night. I remembered the slurring of his voice, and the way his eyes had taken on a glassy look—

A sudden thought made me catch my breath. I sat motionless, dimly aware that Chad had gone back to "shee-shee-sha-*boom*-cha," facing away from us now, thin backside waving seductively beneath the red-and-white tablecloth.

How soon could I get out of here and return to the guest cottage?

Chad exited, to hearty applause, through the archway into the dining room. As soon as he came back, divested of my wedgies and the tablecloth and the wax fruit, the wife of the harmonica player said,

"Don and I had better call it a night, folks. Six o'clock comes awfully early."

"If you'll excuse me I'll go too," I said to my mother. "I still haven't caught up on my sleep."

I kissed her and Chad and Jennifer and went out to the Chevy. Ben Solway accompanied me. A moon approaching its full was up, still near enough to the horizon to have a golden cast. As we went down the walk, Ben looked at me through that yellowish light and said, "I was watching you tonight. There's something on your mind, isn't there?"

I said, wanting nothing but to get away, "Not particularly. I'm just tired, that's all."

He opened the door for me, and I slid behind the wheel. He said, leaning down to look at me, "I think there is something. Did you have a fight over the phone with that guy in New York?"

I said nothing, just inserted the key in the ignition and started to turn it. He put his hand over mine. "So you have quarreled with him. Does that mean there's a chance for me?"

I looked at his face. Such a nice face. Maybe in time, if Mike really had turned away from me . . .

But right then my need to get to that playroom overwhelmed every other consideration. "Ben, I don't know. I like you a lot, I always have. But tonight I'm too tired to think."

He removed his hand, and I turned the ignition key.

By the time I reached the guest cottage, my fingers were so shaky with nervous tension that I had trouble unlocking the front door. I didn't even go up to my

159

bedroom to take off my coat. Instead I walked straight back along the silent hall, through the kitchen, and down those stairs.

I touched the switch. Amber lamps bloomed on the paneled walls. I looked swiftly around the room at the bar, the wide daybed with its brown corduroy cover, the drum set and the guitar which, three nights earlier, someone had sent crashing to the floor. Then I went over to the line of hi-fi equipment which stretched along the wall opposite the daybed.

Beside one of the speakers was a mahogany cabinet about three feet high in which Neil had kept his tapes. I didn't even bother with the top drawers. They were filled, I knew, with tapes of various sorts—Mexican music, some country and western, some rock—which he had bought at record shops in Harlsburg and Tucson. The bottom drawer held blank tapes as well as tapes that he himself had made, some from radio programs, some from albums owned by friends of his. He also had recorded his own singing voice, accompanied by guitar, and a few of his frenetic drum solos.

Fleetingly I thought of him sitting over there behind that drum set, dark hair falling over his damp forehead, eyes glassy, drumsticks flying. Then I gave my full attention to the tapes in the bottom drawer. The labeled ones I left alone. I was sure that the tape I sought would not be labeled.

The first unlabeled tape I threaded onto the spindles unwound with nothing but a faint hissing sound. After less than a minute I took it off, put on another.

160

This one held the old Abbott and Costello "Who's on first" routine, probably recorded from some radio program before I met him. For some reason, he hadn't labeled it. The third tape I put on was another blank. But the fourth—

It had unwound with that hissing sound for only a few seconds when Neil's voice said, "Carla, darling, Carla, sweetheart. I've called again and again, but your friend Althea won't let me speak to you. I guess you know I drove up to Tucson yesterday. That big bruiser Althea's married to wouldn't let me in the door, and he threatened to call the cops if I showed up there again. I'm mailing you this because it's the only way I can think of getting in touch with you."

Sitting rigid, I realized when he had made this tape. It had been during the second year of our marriage. After a particularly violent quarrel, I had fled to my friend Althea and her husband in Tucson, taking ten-month-old Melissa with me, and hiding two black eyes behind dark glasses.

"Come back to me, Carla. Come back to me, you and Melissa both. Everything will be different from now on. I swear it, darling."

My whole body felt chilled. The last time I had heard those words I had been holding a phone to my ear in my darkened Manhattan bedroom. And in this basement room nearly a continent away some-one had been holding the extension phone close to this tape deck, waiting to hang up at just the right moment, and in the meantime smiling, smiling . . .

Neil's recorded voice went on, reminding me of

161

good times we had had, and pleading for forgiveness. And then came words I remembered from that second phone call.

"Carla, honey, I know that I hit you, but it was only because I was drunk. And I'm not going to drink anymore. Oh, I'm having a few tonight, but after this I go on the wagon. So come back, darling."

The pleading voice went on, becoming more and more slurred. Now and then a pouring sound told me that he was refilling his glass. Then he said, with drunken dignity, "If you feel you have to stay away a little longer, I won't insist. But I just had an idea, darling. When you do come back, don't come to the house. Let's meet up by the river. Remember how it used to be before we were married? Remember that night up there when we first made love? There was a full moon—"

It was at that point that I, back in my apartment, had cried, "Neil! Where are you?" And in response that faceless, smiling person in this basement playroom had hung up.

But the voice on the tape went on, often repeating itself now. Sometimes it was almost unintelligible. Finally it trailed off into a mumble and then stopped. The tape went on unwinding, silent except for that faint hiss.

With nerveless fingers I turned off the machine. Why hadn't he mailed that tape to me in Tucson? Perhaps he had been so drunk that the next day he hadn't remembered making it. Or perhaps there had been no need to send it. Perhaps he had made it only the night before he did manage to get me

162

on the phone. Althea had gone out, and I answered the phone, and it was Neil, cold sober and pleading with me.

He drove up to Tucson that afternoon, and Melissa and I drove back with him. Why did I go back? I'm not sure. But I was still rather young, only twenty-two, and doubtful about whether I could make a living for Melissa and myself. Besides, I still loved him at least a little, enough to hope that he would give up drinking.

But he had not. Instead, more than a year later, he had tumbled drunkenly into that river and had been swept to what everyone thought was his death among the rocks below the falls.

And later on, someone had discovered this tape. How much later? I had no way of knowing. I only knew that someone had found it, someone who hated me. I could imagine him playing the tape over and over again, until he knew at just what point to start it when I answered that phone nearly three thousand miles away.

Whoever he had been, he was still out here, not back in New York. I was sure of it. For one thing, there was that feeling of mine which Mike had scorned, the feeling that my persecutor was somewhere near. For another, there was the fact that only three nights ago someone had crawled through a basement window and entered this room, only to retreat after he had knocked over the drum set and the guitar.

I was sure he had come here with the intention of taking the tape. But why? Because he feared I

163

might find it? No, that must have seemed to him a very remote possibility indeed. More likely, he had planned to thread it onto some other tape deck and then, in the early-morning hours, telephone this house.

I rewound the tape, played it again. When the recorded voice suggested that we meet up by the river, a sudden thought made me hold my breath. "Remember that night up there when we first made love? There was a full moon—"

Tomorrow night there would be a full moon, the first full moon since I had returned to Arizona.

Could it be that the night caller would be waiting for me up there tomorrow night?

Heartbeat heavy and rapid now, I thought it through. In all probability he had no idea that I had found this tape, nor that I had discovered Neil to be alive. I had told no one, no one at all except Mike Trenton, about my trip across the border to that cantina in Todos Santos.

No, as far as my tormentor knew, I was still desperate with uncertainty as to whether my husband was alive or dead, and whether I had heard his voice or some impersonator's on my phone back in New York. And he might feel that I, driven by my anxiety to come all the way out here, might be willing to take a further step.

I might accept that invitation to meet my husband up there on the very spot where we had spent our last day together.

And if that was his hope, and if I did go up there, what would happen? Would he be content to amuse himself by watching from some hidden spot as I stood, taut with mingled fear and expectation, in the moonlight? Or would he choose to let me know at long last who he was?

It seemed to me that to a deranged mind—and I had little doubt about his derangement—that spot where my husband had plunged into the deadly torrent would seem a peculiarly appropriate place for him to reveal himself to me and taunt me with my own gullibility and his cleverness.

And if he turned out to be, not just sly and twisted, but downright dangerous?

Well, I would just have to run that risk. To take a policeman or anyone else up there with me would be to defeat my own purpose. The person whose identity I so desperately needed to know would just remain hidden until we left.

And anyway, I had that gun, Neil's gun.

But even with the gun, would I have the courage to go up there?

I had to have that much courage. Too much depended on it for me to lose courage now. Melissa's future safety and my own. My chance of happiness with Mike.

But just the thought of going up there had filled me with cold unease. Before I left the belowground level I opened the door into the rest of the basement and turned on the caged overhead light. The three windows were still closed and locked. On the first floor I checked all doors and windows. Only then did I go upstairs to bed.

19

THERE WAS really no need for my headlights. The flood of radiance from that full moon, now high in the deep blue sky, was so brilliant that I could have driven without lights along the road that ran arrow-straight across the desert floor. Not only bits of glass strewn along the roadsides glittered in that blue-white light, but even the trunks and twisted branches of creosote bushes. In the distance the Azul Mountains were like a jagged cardboard cutout. I knew that as I neared them they would change color to deep purple, fading to dark blue in their folds. But right now they appeared inky black.

For me the day had seemed interminably long. I had not even finished dressing that morning when Martha Baron telephoned, asking me to have coffee with her "around ten o'clock." In her living room we sipped coffee from translucent Sèvres cups and discussed the weather and my latest telephone chat with Melissa. Then she said, "I do feel I should apolo-

166

gize for not having come down to greet your friend the other night. A Mr. Turner, I believe Molly said."

"Trenton, Michael Trenton."

"I was already undressed when he arrived. Besides, I was quite tired that evening. But I trust you did see him."

"Yes. He waited for me in the guest cottage driveway."

"I gathered from Molly that he is a nice-looking man."

"I would say so."

She leaned toward me slightly. "My dear, I don't mean to pry. But is this Mr. Trenton a special friend?"

In my view, she had every right to pry. Any man I married would become her granddaughter's stepfather. "Yes. In fact, he wants to marry me."

At least he had wanted to, I thought unhappily. If there was a time limit on his offer, and I feared there was, perhaps it had already expired.

"And do you think you will marry him?"

"I'm not sure."

"May I ask what sort of work he does?"

"He's on the staff of *Nation's Week.*"

"Oh, a journalist."

Something in her tone made me think that her concept of journalists dated from *The Front Page,* with its cast of bawdy and drunken reporters. To reassure her I said, "He just had an offer to teach at the Columbia School of Journalism."

"I see. Well, my dear, he sounds as if he might be a very good choice for you."

Her gaze went past me, and I knew that she was looking at Neil's portrait. Her patrician features were, as almost always, well controlled, but I was freshly reminded of what grief she felt, and would always feel. I had an almost irresistible impulse to cry out, "Your son is alive!"

But I'd had that out with myself. For her sake, as well as my own, it was best to let her think of him as dead. She would be spared the knowledge of what her son had become. And I would be able to remain fairly sure that Neil would keep his promise about the divorce.

I left her soon after that and drove into town to help my mother and Chad clean up the house after the previous night's celebration. In midafternoon Jennifer called, and each of us in turn chatted with her for a few minutes about the party.

Since Mahlon's was a night job, I had feared he might be hanging around that afternoon, ostensibly to help with the cleaning up, but more likely because he knew I found his presence upsetting. When I finally asked about him, though, my mother said he'd driven off "somewhere or other" before noon.

As I took down paper streamers and scrubbed an ice cream stain off the dining room rug, and, later on, tried to eat roast beef left over from the night before, only my physical being was there in my mother's house. In thought I was already up there on the moon-drenched bank of that turbulent river.

At last supper was over, and I was able to leave. I drove back to the guest cottage and changed to jeans and a denim jacket. I waited for the last of the sunset light to fade from the west and for that enormous moon to rise in the east. I took the little gun from the drawer of the bedside stand and put it in my jacket pocket. Shortly before ten I drove past the main house, its every window dark, and turned toward the mountains. No town stood along this road, or gas stations, or even farmhouses. Thus there was practically no traffic. I met only two other cars, both of them recreational vehicles.

I was close enough now that the mountains had taken on that purple shade familiar to me from nights of full moonlight all through my growing-up years. But tonight the scene's beauty had no power to move me.

When I entered the foothills the road, ruler-straight until then, became a series of curves, some almost hairpin sharp. I passed the entrance to the side road that led to Jennifer's school and then continued on. The tang of creosote bush and sage and juniper growing on the lower slopes gave way to the fragrance of pine. Soon the road was walled in by tall trees whose branches, almost touching, shut out all but a ragged ribbon of moonlight. Heart pounding now, I finally turned onto a much narrower road, little more than a track.

And then, quite suddenly, I was there in the little clearing beside the savage river, its foaming rapids blue-white in the moonlight. It was here, on a blanket spread over pine needles, that Neil and I had first made love. And it was from this spot, three years later, that I had seen a drunken Neil tumble from a rock into the turbulent water.

169

I turned off the ignition and then sat there, hands gripping the wheel. I strained my ears for the slightest sound. On this still night there was not even the sough of wind. The trees which walled the clearing stood motionless, black in the moonlight. The only sound was that of rushing water. And yet, almost as surely as if I had heard the snapping of a twig or the rustle of disturbed branches in the underbrush, I had a sense of someone nearby, waiting.

Waiting for what? For me to get out of my car?

Minutes passed. My tension grew. Then, because I knew that if I waited much longer I would lose my nerve entirely, and wheel the car around and drive away, and thus lose perhaps forever my chance of facing my tormentor—because of all that, I swung the car door back. I got out onto the needle-strewn ground, dimly aware that my legs felt weak, and closed the door. Despite the river's rushing noise, the metallic sound of the door's closing seemed loud.

Hand clutching the gun in my pocket, I stood motionless for a moment there in the pines' deep shadow. No sound except the river's. Plainly, whoever was in hiding somewhere near was waiting for me to make some further move. Feeling the coolness of sweat on my forehead and upper lip, I moved into the clearing's moonlit center, walked to the river's edge, and halted.

Somewhere nearby a car door creaked open and then closed. I whirled in the direction of the sound.

Swish of branches in the underbrush. I saw a tall figure emerge from the pines into their black shadow and then into the moonlight.

170

Mike Trenton.

For several seconds I felt nothing at all. Then memory engulfed me, memory of times when questions about Mike Trenton had formed in my mind, only for me to brush them aside.

My nightmare in that Vermont inn, for instance. How had he known it concerned my husband? Later, when I asked him about it, he had said that he had heard me say something that sounded like "knee," and so had concluded that I had been trying to say Neil's name. But even though I could recall trying to scream in my nightmare, I did not remember making any such sound.

Too, there was that rush of intuitive fear I had felt when, returning from my trip to Mexico, I had found him waiting beside the guest cottage in the predawn dark.

But most damning of all was his presence here. I had told him nothing about that third telephone call, except that it had occurred. And I had told him nothing at all about that tape. In fact, I myself had not discovered the tape until after my last meeting with him. Yet somehow he had known what was on it. And, knowing, he had realized that in my desperation to learn the identity of my tormentor, I might indeed decide to drive up here on this moon-flooded night.

How had he known all that? The answer was sickeningly, paralyzingly obvious. Somehow he had found that tape before I had, at least several months before. Found it, and used it.

For a moment my sense of betrayal was like a

171

bitter taste in my mouth. Then all coherent thought was swallowed up by my terror of that advancing figure.

I jerked the little gun from my pocket. "Stop! Stop right there."

He halted. "Carla—"

I heard my own voice, thin with hysteria. "I've got a gun! And I'll use it."

"No, you won't. Put it away, Carla."

He was moving toward me again. I aimed at his legs and tried to shoot but nothing happened and he was still coming at me. Again I tried, but still the gun didn't work. Now he was only twenty feet or so away. Blind with terror, I turned and raced to the car. I dropped the gun into my pocket with one hand and with the other jerked the car door open. I slid behind the wheel.

Apparently surprise had made him halt for a moment, but now he was coming after me again. I switched on the ignition and drove straight at him.

I saw him jump aside, heard him give a hoarse shout. Then I made a U-turn and flicked on my headlights, and was driving along that narrow track through the pines toward the road.

I had almost reached it when I saw, in the rearview mirror, the lights of his car. I turned left and started down that winding road, my lights tunneling through the darkness beneath the almost interlaced branches and shining on pine trunks at the curves.

It was still almost impossible for me to believe that Mike Trenton had been responsible for those early-morning phone calls. Mike, whom I'd hoped to marry. But he had been. How he had done it, and why, I did not know. But he had.

What a fool I had been to come up here alone! True, if I had turned to the Baronsville police, they would have insisted upon driving up here in one or both of their official cars, perhaps even with ceiling lights flashing. But Ben—dear Ben, whom I should have married long ago—would have helped me on my own terms. Crouched behind the Chevrolet's front seat, he would have remained hidden until that tall figure appeared . . .

But I must not give rein to my pain and bitterness, or think about what I should have done. I had to concentrate all my attention on getting to Baronsville and the safety of the police station.

Mike Trenton's lights were closer now. I speeded up, whipped around a curve. The car's rear end slewed dangerously toward the left-hand side of the road and the steep drop below. I slowed only momentarily. Whatever car he drove was bigger than my rented Chevy, and probably faster. Better to risk shooting off the road than allow him to force me into the cliffside.

Then I realized that I perhaps had another alternative. Just beyond a curve about a mile ahead was the entrance to the road that led to the mission school. If I could turn off there without him realizing it . . .

I whipped around another curve, far faster than was safe. Ahead was a comparatively straight stretch of road. I saw his lights appear around the curve behind me several seconds later than I had expected.

173

I thought, with savage triumph, he was afraid to take that one as fast as I did. Thank God I had driven that road from the age of sixteen onward. I knew, as he did not, where it was merely dangerous to take a curve fast and where it was downright suicidal.

He was gaining on this straight stretch, though. I went around the next curve so fast that the wheels bounced sickeningly. But there was only one more curve between me and the entrance to the mission road. If I could get around it safely . . .

I did. About twenty yards farther on I turned sharply left onto the mission school road. No pines at this lower altitude, but ahead was a stand of juniper. Foot almost to the floorboard, I drove a teeth-jarring hundred yards or so and then stopped in the little grove of trees. I turned off the lights and the ignition, and waited.

After less than a minute I saw his car lights passing along the main road.

I crossed my arms on the steering wheel then, and lowered my head, and for a little while gave myself up to the luxury of tears, tears of fright and bewilderment and humiliation and heartbreak. Then I drove on.

How soon would he realize that I had turned off somewhere? Not until he reached the desert floor, if then. And if he did finally retrace his route, and notice this inconspicuous little side road, and follow it to the mission school, by then it would not matter. I would be safe behind the school's barred wooden gate. And the Baronsville police, summoned by Jennifer and me, would either be there or on their way.

20

As usual, the high wooden gates stood open. Beyond them, across the barren yard, rose the mission school's stucco facade, dark except for the lights in the windows of Jennifer's second-floor office and adjoining bedroom. I drove into the yard, got out, slammed the car door. The sound was loud in the silence. I raced back to the heavy wooden gates, pushed them closed, and thrust the stout iron bar into place. I rested for a moment, breathing heavily, hands clutching the bar. Then I turned and hurried toward the school's entrance.

I had almost reached it when the door opened and Jennifer stepped out in the flood of moonlight. Fleetingly I was aware that she hadn't yet started preparations for bed. She still wore her workday costume of chinos with a khaki shirt hanging free over her waistline, and her brown braids still encircled her head.

"Carla! What is it?"

"It's Mike! Mike Trenton." Shivering now, I crossed my arms in front of me and grasped my forearms.

"That man in New York? The one you think you'll—"

"He's not in New York!" My voice rose. "He's here. He was waiting up by the river—"

"Shhh. We don't want to wake up the kids." She put her arm around me. "Come upstairs, honey. You can tell me about it up there."

When we entered the building I saw that she must have left her office door open because light spilled down onto the ground floor. She limped ahead of me up the stairs, and I followed her into the familiar office with its rolltop desk, walls hung with crayoned drawings and watercolors made by her pupils, beat-up leather couch where she sometimes took brief rests, and a hot plate on which she cooked midafternoon snacks for herself.

"Now sit down," she said, in the soothing voice I had heard her use with upset pupils, "and tell me about it."

Still trembling, I sank onto the couch. She sat down in the swivel chair beside the rolltop. "All right. Go ahead."

"Those phone calls I got in New York. The early-morning ones I told you about. Mike made them. He played this tape over the phone. Parts of it, I mean."

"Carla, what on earth—"

"I don't know how he did it. I'm sure he didn't come out here to play it each time. He must have

176

gotten a copy of it somehow and had it with him in New York—"

"Carla, for heaven's sake! Slow down, and try to speak more clearly. Now what do you mean by 'it'?"

"A tape recording. Neil must have made it about five years ago, that time I took Melissa and went up to Tucson and stayed several days with Althea and her husband. Remember?"

She nodded. "I remember your going up there."

"Neil made the tape while I was away. He must have been very drunk when he did it, because he doesn't even remember making it." My voice rose high and thin. "At least he didn't mention it. But somehow Mike Trenton knew about it and got hold of it—"

"Take it easy, honey, take it easy." Then, after a moment: "You're just not making sense, Carla. You said that Neil doesn't even remember making the tape. Of course he doesn't remember that, or anything." Her voice became gentle. "Neil drowned four years ago. You know that, Carla."

"But he didn't! He's alive, Jennifer. I talked to him just a few nights ago."

She looked at me, hazel eyes under her scanty brows shocked and incredulous. Then she said, "Look, dear. I'm going to make us some cocoa." Long ago I had learned that for Jennifer, cocoa is what chicken soup is supposed to be for Jewish mothers, a remedy for any human misfortune.

"And while I'm making it, you can tell me about seeing Neil." She limped over to the hot plate and, back to me, turned a switch.

177

"It—it started when I heard a noise in the play-room. I went down there and saw that someone must have climbed in through an unlocked window in the basement. . . ."

Dimly aware that she was taking a paper carton of milk and a jar of cocoa from the small refrigerator beside the hot plate, I went on to tell her of finding the postcard photograph of Neil and that sad little Mexican girl.

"I decided that if Neil was alive he might be in Mexico, and that this town named Los Arboles might be the place to start looking for him."

I went on, telling her about Todos Santos, noisy with fiesta, and about finding Neil in the first cantina I came to.

Jennifer took a small saucepan down from its hook above the hot plate. "And you say you actually talked to him?"

From her tone I could not tell whether or not she thought that Neil and the cantina had any existence outside my own mind. Certainly when I called her from New York she had seemed to believe, at least at first, that those early-morning phone calls were simply a fantasy of mine.

"Yes! I sat opposite him at a table in that cafe and talked to him for at least an hour, just as surely as I am talking to you now."

"But, Carla!" She had begun to stir the cocoa. "How is it he didn't drown? And how did he get down to this place—what's the name of it?"

"Todos Santos."

I told her the story Neil had told me, the story

of how, battered but still alive, he had managed to drag himself from the river. I told her about the susceptible divorcée with whom he had gone to Mexico and of how, once there, he had quarreled with her and then just drifted around by himself, living off money he had extracted in the past from his mother.

"And I'm sure he's lived off various women too, Jennifer. One of them came into the cantina not long before I left."

The cocoa must have been done by then, but she went on stirring. "This tape you mentioned. Did you find it before or after you drove to Mexico?"

Her question made me feel, with a rush of relief, that she believed me, or at least was beginning to.

"Afterward. It was Chad's Carmen Miranda act night before last that suddenly made me realize that there might be such a tape. I knew Neil had made a tape of himself singing 'Down Mexico Way' and some other songs. And so after I got home I looked in that little tape cabinet in the playroom and finally found it—"

"Slow down, honey. You're talking too fast again."

I took a deep breath. "What I'd heard over the phone in New York had been only bits of the tape, bits that made no mention of Tucson or Althea. And the last bit was about how wonderful it would be if we could meet up there by the river, with the full moon shining the way it was one night years and years ago, before we even—"

"Easy, Carla, easy." She took down two heavy brown mugs from the shelf above the hot plate. "And

179

so that is why you went up there tonight."

"Yes. I knew I was taking a dreadful chance. But I had this gun of Neil's I'd found on a closet shelf in what used to be our bedroom. And I couldn't pass up any chance of finding out who it was who'd been playing those tapes, so I went up there and Mike got out of the car he'd hidden somewhere in the trees and he came toward me and the gun wouldn't work—"

"Carla!" Then, quietly: "Does he know you came here?"

"I don't think so. I saw him drive past right after I'd turned onto the side road. But oh, Jennifer! We should call the police. I meant to tell you right away that we should call them, but I forgot—"

"We will in a minute. I don't think there's any danger right now. Even if he did somehow manage to track you here, I don't think he'd try to batter those gates down or do anything else violent, not with seventeen children here to witness it."

Turning from the hot plate, she handed me a mug of cocoa. "Take a sip of that."

I did. "Good," I said mechanically, although for me it had no taste at all.

She said, "Now let's have a look at that gun."

I drew the gun from my pocket, handed it to her. She said, with a touch of amusement in her voice, "No wonder it wouldn't work. You forgot to take off the safety. Now how could a girl raised in the Southwest make a mistake like that?" She laid the gun beside the hot plate.

"I don't know. I guess when I saw Mike Trenton

180

coming at me, I was so confused and panic-stricken that I couldn't think."

"Of course you couldn't." She took a sip of cocoa and then set the mug down beside the hot plate. "Now go in the bedroom and lie down."

"But the police—"

"I'll call them. Go in the bedroom. Take your cocoa with you."

Obediently, I went into the little room, which, with its narrow bed covered by a Navajo blanket, its dressing table bare of everything except a comb and brush, had always reminded me of a nun's cell. A lamp, its bulb of thriftily low wattage, burned on the little stand beside the bed. To try to read by it would be to risk blindness. But then, Jennifer had always said that beds were for sleeping, not reading.

I kicked off my shoes and lay down.

21

FROM HER office came the sound of my sister dialing
the phone. After an interval I heard her say, "Is
that you, Floyd?" Floyd Daitch was a member of
Baronsville's four-man police force. "Yes, Jennifer
Jackson. Could you come up here to the school right
away? . . . It's too long to tell you over the phone,
but my sister's here, and we both feel we need protection. . . . If you can bring Danny Crisp along it
might be a good idea. . . . Fine. Thanks a lot, Floyd."

She came in and sat down beside the bed, with
the lamplight shining dimly on her thin face. "They'll
be here as soon as they can. Now where is this Todos
Santos, exactly?"

I told her.

"And this woman of his who came into the cantina.
What did she look like?"

Puzzled as to why she should ask such a question,
I said, "Oh, I guess she was in her middle or late

182

thirties. She was tall, and very thin, and wore lots of makeup."

"How was she dressed?"

Still puzzled, I said, "A yellow blouse, low cut. And a tight skirt. Black, I think. Yes, black."

Jennifer's lip curled. "Just a common whore, and not even good-looking. She can't mean a thing to him."

For a moment there was no room in my mind for anything but bewilderment. I watched, uncomprehending, as the scornful triumph in her face gave way to a soft, joyous look. "So he's alive. Only about a hundred miles away, and alive."

I lay with my gaze riveted on her face, still not understanding, only aware that the woman who sat beside me was not the Jennifer Jackson I'd known, or thought I'd known, all my life. This woman was a stranger.

She was looking at me. That scornful triumph was coming back into her face. "You never guessed, did you? You had no idea that I loved him long before you did. Oh, sure, I suppose he barely realized that I was alive. Just the same, I was in love with him while you were still a kid in high school."

Her voice turned bitter. "And if you hadn't let him bring you back from Tucson that time five years ago, I think I could have made him love me too, really love me."

I said, stunned, "Are you talking about Neil, Jennifer? *Neil?*"

"Yes, Neil! Oh, I know what you're thinking. Plain

old Jennifer, with her bad leg. How could she ever have had the nerve to even think Neil Baron might look at her? But he did! I was with him the night he made that tape."

"With Neil?" I asked dazedly. "In the playroom?"

"Yes! I knew you'd run off to Tucson, taking Melissa with you, and so I went that night to—to tell him how sorry I was, or at least that's what I *did* tell him. He invited me down to the playroom— me, old maid Jennifer!—and we had some drinks, and then he got the idea of making a tape he could mail to you, since he hadn't been able to either phone you or see you. And he did make it, with me sitting there."

I could visualize it. My husband, drunk and maudlin to the point of tears, speaking into the recorder there in that expensive, amber-lighted playroom. And Jennifer watching him with that same hungry look that had leaped into her face moments ago when she said, "I loved him long before you did!"

Now she said, her chin lifting, "And when he'd made the tape and put it in that cabinet, he and I made love!"

I thought of them there on the daybed in the amber glow. Jennifer, not just willing but eager to sacrifice her virginity to the wellborn and handsome man she had loved so hopelessly for so long. And Neil, probably too blind drunk at that point to know anything except that here was a female body, affording him momentary surcease from his self-pity and injured self-esteem.

"If you'd stayed away, I could have made him fall

in love with me. I know I could have. Oh, don't laugh."

I hadn't laughed, or smiled, or moved, or done anything except lie there. And even though I wasn't afraid of her—not really; not yet—something warned me that I had better be as quiet, as passive, as possible.

Jennifer said, "I had a lot more than just a body to offer him. I had a good mind, a *really* good mind. And I loved him more than you ever could have. But he went to Tucson the very next day, and you came back with him. . . ."

She leaned toward me slightly. "Yes, you were right. He didn't remember making that tape. About a month after you came back from Tucson I saw him in a booth in Eddie's Diner. I walked in and sort of invited myself to sit with him. He was polite enough, ordered me some coffee and all, but when I mentioned the night before you came back from Tucson he gave a sort of embarrassed laugh and said, 'I'm afraid I was sort of drunk that night. I remember your coming to the house and saying how sorry you were that Carla and I were having trouble. And I remember our going down to the playroom for a drink. I'm afraid I don't remember anything after that. But I guess you managed to find your way out all right.' "

Her voice became bitter. "I said that yes, I'd managed to find my way out."

In my embarrassment and pity, I had almost forgotten my own plight. I asked, "Why have you finally decided to tell me all this?"

The hazel eyes in the thin face looked down at me coldly. "Because I want to make sure you know how much I've always hated you."

"Jennifer!"

"You're surprised. But if you had ever bothered to give my life more than a thought or two, you wouldn't be."

"Jennifer, I've always thought of how—how brave and wonderful you've been—"

"Brave and wonderful! Of course, when you're a cripple with a plain face, what other role is there for you except to be—admirable. Noble, generous Jennifer, who does so much good despite her handicap! In high school I had no hope of becoming the sort of popular girl you were later on, so I made myself useful to the girls who *were* popular. I wrote their themes and did their geometry problems until they took me into their club, where I could at least have the illusion of popularity.

"In college I had hopes for a while of that young minister marrying me. Not that I loved him. Even back then I knew that Neil Baron was the only man I could ever love. But I'd have been glad to marry Richard. That was his name, remember? Richard Atwood.

"But he married someone else," she went on. "So after graduation I turned to Good Works." Her sardonic tone seemed to capitalize the phrase.

I said, still feeling dazed and almost incredulous, "I always thought you liked running this school."

"Oh, it's better than teaching in a public school, where I would have a lot of sound-in-wind-and-limb colleagues to remind me of what I am. And these Indian kids are politer and quieter than public school kids. Maybe it's because they suffer from the same sort of chronic depression that afflicts a lot of adult Indians, but anyway, they're pretty easy to manage. For some reason, though, people think it's quite wonderful of me to isolate myself up here in the hills in a mission school. When I go through Baronsville, wearing my bonnet, everyone's polite and respectful. There's even that medal the Society of Friends gave me. But believe you me, a medal doesn't do much to warm you in bed on a cold night."

The bitter voice ceased. After a moment I said, "I never dreamed— But now I can see how you might feel the way you do."

I broke off, and then blurted out, "But Jennifer! How can you say you've always hated me? What did I ever—"

"You were born, that's what you did! How do you think that made me feel? Oh, I'd already been aware of being lame. Neighborhood kids made sure of that. And I knew that Mama and Dad weren't my real parents. But at least they were all mine. Then, when I was five, you were born. I think Mama and Dad tried to make me feel that there was no difference between us, but of course there was. You were *theirs*. Besides, you were cute and pretty, and on your way to being a champion swimmer even before you started school, thanks to that instructor they had at the high school pool in the summertime. And you used to dance. You'd turn on the radio and dance around the living room, and I'd see our parents

187

watching you with that proud, besotted look on their faces—"

She broke off and then said, "I tried to kill you when you were five."

I looked at her, stunned and unbelieving. She said, "Mama and Dad were visiting some people up the street. I pushed you into that upstairs hall closet and locked the door. I thought that by the time they got back you'd have smothered to death."

I said, feeling sick, "You've got it all wrong, Jennifer. It was Mahlon who locked me in that closet. He came up behind me and shoved me in and locked the door—"

"I was the one who came up behind you. Mahlon was out in that tree house of his. But I knew that when they found you dead, and Mahlon denied doing it, and I denied doing it, it would be me they'd believe.

"Only you didn't die," she went on in a flat voice. "Mama and Dad had forgotten something, and so they came back too soon, while you were still kicking the door and screaming."

Not Mahlon who had induced in me my lifelong fear of enclosed places. Jennifer.

For the first time I felt, not just bewilderment and embarrassment and pity, but fear. She and I might as well have been alone there. The dormitories where her pupils lay asleep were on that same floor but at the other side of the building, separated from my sister's quarters by a small inner courtyard.

"You told them Mahlon had locked you in the closet," Jennifer was saying. "Naturally you thought that. He was always playing mean little tricks on you, the sort of tricks I was too smart to play. Young as I was then, I'd realized it was best to hide what I felt.

"Mahlon denied locking you in, but neither Mama nor Dad believed him. Mama telephoned Mahlon's father to come and get him, and he didn't visit us again for, oh, maybe a year. Remember?"

I shook my head. I remembered only those nightmarish moments in the dark closet, not their aftermath.

I managed to say, "That tape. Was it you—"

"Yes!"

I said, feeling sick, "You're the one who made those calls to me at three and four in the morning? Oh, Jennifer! What a terrible—"

"You deserved to be punished for what you did! You just stood there on the riverbank and watched him drown. You, a champion swimmer. Oh, I know now that he didn't drown. But it's no thanks to you that he's alive."

It wasn't like that, I wanted to say. It was a kind of paralysis that held me for several seconds. And when I finally was able to pick up that branch, it was too late.

But she knew about that. I'd told the police that, and the coroner, and Neil's mother, and everyone else. If Jennifer hadn't believed me then, words would do me no good now.

Besides, I thought, again with that little ripple of fear down my body, Jennifer was beyond reach of rational argument. For more than a quarter of a cen-

189

tury, behind that calm, even sweet mask of hers, she had harbored jealousy and bitter hate and a hopeless love. And year after year those hidden emotions had taken their toll on her.

The mask was off now. I thought, as I looked up into those eyes that seemed to actually glitter in the light from the bedroom lamp, she's quite mad.

"You deserved punishment! But instead, what happened? You went to New York, and you got a good job. And as if that weren't enough, you met this man. I remember you burbling over long distance about how handsome he was, bright, and successful, and all-around wonderful. It was then that I got the idea about the tape."

"You—you knew it was still there, in the playroom?"

"I only hoped so. After all, Neil might have destroyed it. When I first got the idea of looking for it, I couldn't. Some people from Virginia, family connections of Martha Baron's, were staying in the guest cottage. But when I heard they'd left I decided to risk it. I drove down there one night, very late, and left my car out on the road. Then I walked back to the cottage. The front and back doors were locked, but I found a basement window unlocked, and I opened it and crawled in. It wasn't easy. When I dropped onto the floor I almost lost my balance and fell. But I managed not to."

I pictured her limping across that cement floor, a pocket flashlight in her hand, and then opening the door to that paneled room where, one night five

190

years in the past, she'd had her one experience of physical love.

"I'd put several unlabeled tapes on the spindle before I found the right one. I can't tell you what it was like hearing his voice again, and thinking of him as long-since dead, his body wedged under some boulder in that terrible river."

She fell silent for a moment, eyes looking at the opposite wall. Then that bright—far too bright—gaze returned to my face. She said, speaking rapidly now, "I made the first call that same night. I'd found the spot on the tape that was just right. I set the tape to start there, and I dialed your number, and when you answered the phone I turned the machine on."

For the first time I doubted her story. Something didn't make sense. After a moment I realized what it was. "You used that extension phone in the playroom?"

"Of course. Didn't I just tell you?"

"But the call must have shown up on Mrs. Baron's bill! Didn't you realize it would?"

"Of course. But what of it? I'm sure she never sees any bills. Her business manager handles all that. And he wouldn't be surprised at seeing your New York number on her phone bill. In your letters and phone calls to me you sometimes mentioned that Mrs. Baron had called Melissa on her birthday.

"True," she went on, "the guest house has a different phone number than the main house. But I was sure that when old Mr. Farnsworth saw the bill he'd

191

figure that, for one reason or another, she'd been in the guest house when she decided to call you and Melissa."

I believed her then. This woman who all my life I had referred to and thought of as my sister had not just once, but three times, sat there in that empty house late at night and dialed my apartment number. She had wanted to bewilder and terrify me. She had wanted to make me believe that perhaps I had a living husband and therefore had no right to marry Mike Trenton. She had wanted, in her phrase, to punish me, not only for Neil's death, but for having been the object of his love, however ambivalent and unpredictable that love had been. And she had succeeded in punishing me.

I said, "You were in that house a few nights ago, weren't you?"

"The guest house? Yes."

"You were after the tape, weren't you? You were afraid I might look for it and find it."

"I was after the tape, but not because I feared you might find it."

The look she gave me, a look of grudging surprise, told me that all her life she must have thought of me as far less intelligent than herself, certainly not intelligent enough to surmise the existence of that tape.

"I wanted it," she said, "because I'd bought a tape deck. It's right here now, under that bed you're lying on. I liked the idea of phoning you some night at the guest house and playing another section of that tape."

192

Chills rippled down my body at the thought of what it would have been like, there alone in that big house, listening to Neil's voice, and wondering if he might be phoning from somewhere nearby, perhaps even as near as his mother's house.

"But things went wrong that night, and I didn't get the tape," Jennifer said. "I hurt my leg, my game one, while I was crawling in that window. And then in the playroom my leg buckled under me, the way it does sometimes, and I fell against the guitar and those drums and knocked them over. I knew then that I didn't have time to go through those tapes and find the right one. I had to get out of there, as fast as I could, on a leg that was not only lame but hurting like hell. It was all I could do to climb up on that garden chair and crawl out through the window."

"Did you—did you hope to frighten me into going back to New York? By playing that tape, I mean?"

"I intended to frighten you, period. As for your going back to New York, what difference would it have made to me whether you did or didn't?"

After a moment she went on, "As a matter of fact, I wasn't at all surprised when you came out here to Arizona. What did surprise me was that you went up to that spot on the river tonight." Amusement in her voice now. "But thinking back over the last part of that tape, I can see how you might get the notion that there was a chance that whoever had made those calls might be waiting up there for you. But it never occurred to me to go up there."

I said, as quietly as I could, "Jennifer."

"Yes?"

"What are you going to do now?"

"Do? Why go to Neil, of course. He needs me. He's always needed someone like me, a woman intelligent enough to help him work through his problems until he understands *why* he drinks. Once he understands, he'll stop. And I'm sure that now, after all he's been through, he too will realize that he needs me."

I said, trying to sound matter-of-fact, "Yes, perhaps you could help him stop drinking. I think I'll leave now, Jennifer."

I sat up and thrust my feet into my shoes. "When Floyd Daitch comes, you can tell him it was all a mistake. I'm sure that you'll have no trouble thinking up an explanation."

She got up from her chair, took a step backward. "Floyd? You don't still think I actually called the police, do you?"

Some time ago it had occurred to me that probably she had not. It also had occurred to me that she probably had picked up that little gun from beside the hot plate and put it in her pocket. Still, it was a shock to see it suddenly in her hand.

My throat felt dry. "Jennifer, put the gun down."

"Don't be absurd." I heard a click. "The safety catch isn't on now."

"You can't use that gun. Why, you'd wake up the whole school."

"I'll use it if I have to. You believe that, don't you? Yes, I can see by your eyes that you do."

I said, very carefully, "What is it you want of me?"

"I want you to drive us both up to that spot on the river."

"Why?"

"Because you're going to commit suicide up there. You are going into the river at the same spot where Neil did. Remorse had been eating away at you for years, you see. I'll be able to tell a very convincing story about how I pleaded with you, even tried to struggle physically with you, but it was no use. Into the river you went."

Eyes fixed on the ugly little mouth of that gun, I said, "Jennifer—," and then broke off. I had almost said, "Jennifer, be reasonable," and that would have been a very dangerous thing to have said.

"Jennifer, let's discuss this."

"What is there to discuss? You tried to kill Neil. Just standing there when you knew he would almost certainly drown was the same as trying to kill him. So it is only right that you pay for it.

"Besides," she went on, in a matter-of-fact voice, "Neil and I will want to marry, freely and openly. We can't do that if he already has a wife, can we?"

With a weird detachment, I reflected that perhaps Neil *would* want to marry her. It might be that he would see in her a solution to his mother problem. Jennifer, he might feel, would offer him the motherly protection and indulgence he craved, without the motherly domination he feared and hated.

"On your feet, Carla. That's right. And don't entertain any notions about rushing me. True, I'm lame, but I'm taller than you, and perhaps just as strong.

Most important of all, I'm the one holding the gun."

My own voice sounded unfamiliar to me, almost the voice of a stranger. "Jennifer, if you shoot me—"

"Right here? Yes, if I shoot you right here I'll be in trouble. But so will you. And I'll be able to get out of *my* trouble. I'll say that I'd fallen asleep at my desk, and that when you came bursting in I thought you were a burglar. My kids here at the school will believe that. So will everyone else. Do you think that people will doubt the word of Jennifer Jackson, director of the Protestant Sisters' Mission School? Don't be silly."

"But they will doubt you. That gun must be registered to Neil. How will you explain—"

"I'll say that he gave it to me, his sister-in-law, a long time ago for my protection in this isolated place. Who could dispute that, except you, and you won't be able to dispute anything. Now walk ahead of me down the stairs. And don't make any noise."

I found out then that you can't believe in the imminence of your own violent death. At least I could not. Oh, my body did. I felt the cold sweat trickling down my sides under my clothing. I heard the beats of my terrified heart, so rapid that they ran together with a seething sound, like that of distant surf. Still my mind could not grasp the fact that she meant to kill me. I moved down those stairs as if in a dream. Through the seethe of my heartbeats I could hear her uneven footsteps behind me.

At the foot of the stairs my mind began to emerge from its dreamlike numbness. I threw a quick glance to my left along the lower hall. If I could dash down there into the dimmer light, with screams loud enough to reach the dormitories . . .

I don't think I turned my head. Even so, she must have guessed my thought, because I felt the gun prod me between my shoulder blades. "Don't try it, Carla. If I have to, I'll kill you right here. Now go outside."

In my haste to follow my sister up to her office, I had left the front door open. Aware of her right behind me, I stepped out onto barren earth bathed in blue-white brilliance. The moonlight no longer was beautiful. It seemed charged with an ancient evil, a murderous envy that went clear back to Cain.

22

AT HER DIRECTION, I unbarred the high wooden gates. Moving carefully—"Don't try to turn toward me, Carla. Don't even think of it!"—I went back to my rented car and, at her bidding, opened the door beside the driver's seat and the one directly behind it. I slid behind the wheel, aware that almost at the same moment she had sat down in the rear seat. She did not hold the gun against the back of my neck, but I knew it was there, only inches away.

"All right, Carla. Let's go."

With numb fingers I turned on the ignition. I drove out through the gates and down that rutted side road.

We had entered the shadow of the little juniper grove when she asked, "Have you told anyone else about Neil being alive?" From her tone I could tell that she was annoyed with herself for not having asked that question earlier. "Mama and Chad? Mrs. Baron? Anyone?"

Would it be better to tell the truth, or to lie? My mind, still numb, wrestled with the problem.

"Did you hear me, Carla?"

Best to tell the truth. "No, I haven't told anyone. Neil made me promise not to."

"Good!"

It wasn't until then that I realized that the answer I had given was not true, after all. I had told Mike of finding my husband down there in that Mexican town.

I thought of saying, "Mike Trenton knows. I told him only hours after I had talked with Neil. Mike won't believe that guilt drove me to drown myself. Mike will go to the police, and your whole story will collapse."

But with my mind functioning better now, I knew it was too late to say that. She would not believe me. And if she did, she might be enraged enough to kill me right here. Best to keep silent and hope that up there beside the river I could somehow wrest the gun away from her . . .

The river. Mike emerging from the pines to walk toward me. Why had he been waiting for me up there? I knew now that it was not because he had been my night caller, terrifying me with excerpts from that tape. Despite my extremity, I felt a stab of compunction at the thought that, even for a moment, I had considered him capable of doing that to me.

But still, why had he been up there, waiting? How had he known this night of full moonlight might bring me up to the river? Again I reflected that I had never given him any details about that third telephone call. I had told him only that there had been such a call. And so how had he known?

Bleakly I realized that, in about half an hour, the answer to that question would cease to matter to me. Unless I could get that gun away from her . . .

I wondered what she planned to do. Force me at gun point to cross from one boulder to another, as Neil had crossed that long-ago afternoon, until I was out to where the river ran deeply and fiercely? Yes, that probably was it. She would shoot me then and watch me topple into the water. If the shot did not kill me, the river soon would.

After she had hurled the gun as far as she could into the water, she would drive back to Baronsville and tell the police her story. How she'd tried to dissuade her suicidal sister, perhaps even wrestling with me to try to get possession of the gun. ("But Carla was younger than me, and stronger, and besides, I'm lame.") How I'd gotten away from her and, with leaping strides, crossed to that midstream boulder, and shot myself, and toppled into the water.

My body, if it was ever found, would have been so battered by the river that no one would be able to tell whether the bullet had been fired from yards away, or only inches. Yes, I thought, that probably was what she planned as she sat behind me, the gun pointed at the back of my neck.

For the first time, my mind as well as my body accepted the nearness of my own death. I began to feel insensate, as if I were already dead, swept along beneath the river's foaming surface, feeling nothing as the current pounded me against the jagged rocks.

We had reached the junction of the narrow side road with the main one. "Turn here, Carla."

I did not ask which way. I turned right, toward the mountain's crest and the river beyond it. Moments later, I rounded a curve.

Headlights of a descending car moved toward us. My heart gave a sudden, almost painful leap of hope. Mike? When he reached the desert floor, had he realized he must have missed me? Had he turned around, driven back up to the river, and then, finding no trace of me, again turned around?

Then that surge of hope gave way to a new fear. If he slowed as he passed us, and he surely would, what would Jennifer do when she saw Mike Trenton at the wheel? Fire at him?

Relief washed over me. She could not recognize him. She had never met Mike Trenton.

True, she might suspect that the driver of that approaching car was Mike. But on the other hand he might be someone from the ranger's station on the other side of the mountain, or someone returning from a visit to illegal cougar traps he had set, or some young man, his girl beside him, who had driven up into the mountains on this romantically moonlit night.

I tried to slacken speed, just a little. She noticed it. "Don't slow down, Carla. And when that car passes, keep looking straight ahead. Don't try any signaling."

The other car seemed to be slowing. Heartbeat

thunderous, I stared straight ahead as it began to pass us. But from the corner of my eye I was able to glimpse the driver.

It was Mike, with his face turned toward me. Had he also seen Jennifer, seated directly behind me? He must have. Perhaps he had even seen the glint of the gun in her hand. Even if she had lowered it momentarily, he might have suspected from my attitude—body rigid, face turned straight ahead—that I was being threatened by a weapon.

I tried to send him a silent message. Don't try to stop us! Not now. She'll kill us both.

His car looked like the same rented one, a dark two-door, in which he had waited in the guest house driveway the night I came back from that trip into Mexico. He passed us, continued on down the road.

"Was that him?"

"I don't know what you mean."

"Your New York friend, of course."

"No." After a moment I added, "I think it was a man from the ranger station, one of Chad's VFW friends. I met him once, about a year before I went to New York."

Whether she believed that or not I don't know. All she said was, "Drive faster."

"We might—"

"No, we won't go off the road. I know you're too good a driver for that. Now drive faster."

I pressed harder on the accelerator, rounded one curve, then another. No sign of Mike. Could it be that he somehow hadn't realized that I was in very bad trouble? Or had he realized it, but felt he had best get the police to help him? There won't be time, I cried inwardly. I'll be dead up there before you and the police can reach me.

In my rearview mirror I saw headlights, rounding the curve I had taken only moments before.

Jennifer saw them too. For the first time she prodded that gun against the back of my neck. "Faster."

I did speed up, but only as little as I dared. I rounded another curve. A comparatively long straight stretch ahead.

And then suddenly the other car had rounded the curve behind us and was coming fast, fast. It was beside us now, its side grinding with a screech of metal along the Chevrolet's side. Every nerve in my body drawn thin, I turned the wheel sharply toward the embankment.

Even though I had been braced for the impact, my head snapped back. I saw that Mike, his headlights still on, had braked to a stop a few feet away. Then I threw myself sideways onto the seat. My body seemed to shrink in upon itself in anticipation of her leaning over the seat back, firing that gun—

But instead she was waiting for her more dangerous foe. I heard a door open and knew that Mike had gotten out of his car. Terrified for him now, I sat up and saw him hurrying toward us. I screamed, "Mike!" just as the little gun fired. That tall figure kept coming. She fired again. I realized that perhaps this bullet had hit him because he hesitated momentarily. Then he was beside the Chevy's rear door and reaching in.

Grasping the thin wrist of the hand that held the

little gun, he hauled her, screaming, out of the car. Dazed, sick, I watched their unequal struggle out there in the mingled light of the moon and the refracted glow of his headlights.

I saw the gun fall from the hand he held upraised. Perhaps he relaxed momentarily, because she broke free of him. With a strange, wailing sound, almost like that of a wounded animal, she turned and, at a limping run, started down the road.

He picked up the gun, dropped it into his coat pocket, and took two long strides after her.

I cried, "Mike! Let her go!"

He halted. On shaking legs I got out of the car and stood beside him. That thin figure, still at that lurching run, had almost reached the curve in the road. As I watched, all my terror of her, all my rage against her, gave way to an aching pity. What pain and humiliation she must have suffered, from early childhood onward, to make her behave as she had.

And I just could not believe that she had always hated me. There was the time when she was twelve and I was seven, and she had made an evening dress for my Barbie doll because our mother had said she couldn't afford the one I'd seen advertised in a magazine. There was the time when, away at college, she had sent some money to help pay for my high school cheerleader uniform. Surely some of that generosity had been genuine, not just part of an act designed to keep me and the rest of the world from guessing what she really felt. Surely Jennifer had loved me at least a little.

She disappeared around the curve. Something

would have to be done about Jennifer. A person that disturbed could not be left in charge of children. She should at least have some sort of therapy. Yes, something would have to be done. But not right away, not tonight.

23

MIKE SAID, "She's your sister, isn't she?" When we'd first met I had told him about my adoptive sister, so brilliant and hard-working, and so cheerful despite her handicap.

"Yes."

"Why in God's name was she holding a gun on you?"

"I'll tell you later." I saw that his right hand was touching his left shoulder. "Mike! She hit you, didn't she?"

"Just barely." He smiled down at me. "What is it John Wayne used to say? It's only a crease?"

"Nevertheless, I want to look at it, right now."

"All right. I'll get my suitcase out of the car. I've got a first-aid kit in it."

I helped him off with his jacket and shirt. He had been right. The bullet, even though it had penetrated his clothing, had done little more than scrape a bit of skin from his shoulder. While he leaned against his car's front fender I applied iodine and gauze.

And I talked. I told him of finding that tape Neil had made. I told him about Jennifer. About her consuming passion for the man I had married, her desire to punish me for his supposed death, and tonight, after she had learned Neil was alive, her grim determination to get rid of me.

I helped him on with his shirt and coat. He held me close for a moment. Then he asked, "If we can get that Chevrolet started, do you think you can drive it out of these mountains? Just say so if you feel too shaky. We can both go in my car and do something about yours later."

"No, I think I can drive."

He managed to start the Chevrolet and back it away from the embankment. One of its front fenders was bent, but not so badly that it scraped against the tire. He started down the road in his rented car, and I followed in mine.

We passed the entrance, so inconspicuous as to be almost invisible, to that narrow road that led to the mission school. Had she had time to reach the school, or at least the side road? Or had she, somewhere back there along the main road, crouched down under the trees and watched Mike's car and mine drive past?

Mike. I still did not know why he had been waiting for me up by the river tonight.

The road, curving less frequently now, finally reached the desert floor. I sounded my horn and then slowed to a stop at the roadside. Mike backed up, doused his lights, and then walked back through the blue-white moonlight to sit beside me in the Chevy. "What's the trouble?"

"I just can't wait any longer to find out. Mike, I never told you much about that last phone call I received in New York, did I? I mean, I didn't tell you what the caller said."

"No, you didn't."

"And yet you knew what was on the last part of that tape, didn't you?"

"Yes."

"How did you know? How did you know I might drive up there tonight, thinking I might meet the person who had played that tape over the phone?"

"Simple, my darling. It's the power of the press."

When I just looked at him he went on, "After you left New York I realized that you hadn't told me what your caller had said during that third call. Maybe we had been too busy quarreling the last time I saw you there—remember?—but anyway, you didn't tell me. And I felt it was important for me to know as much as I could about the perhaps dangerous person you had come out here to look for.

"Then I remembered that the phone company had recorded that last call. I went to the phone company office. No dice, some jerk behind a desk told me. Such information was confidential. I called the phone company's head of public relations and identified myself as a *Nation's Week* staff member. He fell all over himself. Invited me down to the phone company to listen to those few sentences they had

208

recorded, and handed me a typed transcript of them before I left."

"And you realized that I might drive up to the river—"

"No, not then. All I realized then was that I was getting more and more scared about your safety, and that I'd better fly out here. After I'd waited for hours in the driveway of that damned guest house, only to have you tell me you didn't want me hanging around, I was almost mad enough to take you at your word and fly back to New York. In fact, I even drove to Tucson, checked into a hotel, and reserved a seat on the night flight to New York.

"Then, when I woke up in midafternoon after a few hours' sleep, it suddenly hit me. The full moon was only a couple of nights away. Because of that third telephone call, you might go up to that spot on the river, hoping to meet the man responsible. And he indeed might be there, a man crazed, dangerous—"

"So you decided to be there too."

Mike nodded. "I canceled my plane reservation. Then I went to the newspaper office in Tucson. I lucked out. The reporter who'd covered the story of Neil Baron's drowning was still there. He'd gone with a photographer to that spot on the river, so he was able to tell me exactly where it was.

"I went to a sporting goods store and bought a sleeping bag and a lantern and a few cans of Sterno. I bought some food, too, cheese and cold cuts and bread and eggs and some oranges. Then I drove to

209

the Azul River. I was there last night and all day and again tonight, parked back in the pines. Finally you showed up."

I cried, feeling a stir of remembered terror, "Why didn't you call out as soon as I stopped my car? Then I wouldn't have been afraid. But you didn't even get out of your car until I'd walked down to the river. And when I heard the sound of a car door opening and closing I was sure I was about to see the person who'd made those calls. Then I saw you walking toward me, and I panicked—"

"Easy! Take it easy. Think for a minute, darling. When I heard a car coming, how could I know it was yours? Even after you got out of your car, you stayed back in the pines' shadow. It wasn't until you walked out into the moonlight that I saw it was you.

"I'm sorry, honey," he added. "I'm awfully sorry."

"It's all right. It was silly of me to have lost my head."

He held me close and kissed me. "You'd better get back to that guest house and get some sleep. I'll drive over to— What's the name of that town about fifteen miles from here?"

"Harlsburg."

"I noticed when I passed through it that it has a motel. I'll spend the night there, what's left of it."

Dear Mike! Not just strong, but sensitive too. Sensitive enough to know that I could not bear the thought of our both sleeping in that house where I'd lived for three stormy years with Neil.

He kissed me again. "I'll be back in the morning," he said, "and we'll arrange to fly to New York."

24

As it turned out, we did not fly to New York the next day. A whole week passed before Mike and I boarded, at ten in the morning in Tucson, an east-ward-bound plane.

Most of that week had been taken up with the coroner's hearing, and then the arrangements for Jennifer's funeral.

The morning after she had run, limping, from Mike and me on that moonlit road, two of her girl students, walking down the hall past her office, saw that its door was open. They also heard her phone ringing, unanswered. After a brief consultation, they walked through the empty office and into her bed-room.

Clad in a nightgown and a gray flannel robe, and with her brown hair lying in two neat plaits over her shoulders, she lay stretched out on the Navajo blanket which covered her narrow bed. On the night table beside her stood an empty vial with a label showing that it had contained sleeping pills prescribed for her two weeks earlier by Dr. Wisart, the elderly physician who had brought about half of the present and former population of Baronsville, including Melissa and myself, into the world. After examining her body, Dr. Wisart gave it as his opinion that she had died around three in the morning the night before.

A note had been lying beside the empty sleeping pill bottle. It said:

> Dear Mama and Chad and Carla,
>   Recently I went up to Tucson for a medical examination. You see, if what I suspected was true, I didn't want you to know about it right away.
>   It was true. I have cancer.
>   I simply cannot face it, and so I have chosen to die at my own time and on my own terms.
>   Try to understand. And try to forgive me, not just for what I do now, but for everything else.
>   My love to you,
>   Jennifer

Did she know, or at least hope, that Mike and I would never contradict that note, never tell the truth about her? I like to think that, during those last lonely moments before she took those pills, she felt she could trust me to say nothing.

During the autopsy no cancer was discovered. The whole town was indignant about that. Those Tucson doctors! A lot of quacks and goof-off artists who came out to Arizona from all over the country because they liked the climate and wanted to play golf all

212

the year round. Somebody ought to try to track down the doctor who gave her that diagnosis.

But nobody did try, during those few days after her death. I doubt that anyone ever will. People forget.

There was considerable head-shaking over her note. Why had she asked forgiveness, not just for her suicide, but "for everything else"? What sins could Jennifer Jackson have committed?

Almost everyone in town who was not too young, or too old, or too sick, came to her funeral. Even Martha Baron was there. As I saw the genuine sorrow in their faces, and as I, outside the church afterward, stood in line with Mother and Chad to hear their admiring comments about her, I was more glad than ever that Mike and I had agreed to keep our mouths shut.

Now, as the big plane carried us eastward, Mike and I talked in low voices. He said, "Do you think Neil will ever let his mother know that he is alive?"

"I think it's probable, especially if his luck with women begins to run out. And in time he'll start thinking about all that Baron money. Probably then he'll decide that making sure he inherits will be worth putting up with her for a few years."

"Well, just so he stays down there in that village long enough for us to have the divorce papers served."

"I don't think we have to worry about that."

I leaned back and looked through the window. Thirty thousand feet below our plane the flat farmlands of Kansas seemed to crawl westward. I closed

213

my eyes, acutely aware, although not even our hands were touching, of the man beside me. And I was gratefully aware, too, that with each throb of the giant motors my future with Mike and Melissa grew closer, while all the rest receded farther into the past—that grieving rich woman in her fine house, and her son in that Mexican cantina, and, its foam blue-white in the moonlight, that savage river.